For all the tears we've shed

V J Garland

For all the tears we've shed by V.J.Garland

Published by V.J.Garland
https://vanessajgarland.com/
Copyright © 2024 V.J.Garland

For permissions contact: vgarland89@outlook.com

Book Cover Illustration by Angie Liu
Editor: Allison Johnston-Crozier
Editor: Jasmine Barry

ISBN: 978-1-7635600-0-0

First Edition.

Genre: Adult Romance

Summary: Dane and Stella are riding life's rollercoaster with all the bumps and turns that come with it.
Dane is a newly divorced single dad with 3 girls starting life all over again. He soon learns he's spent too much time away as a SEAL and he needs to relearn who his girls are.

Stella is on the journey of her life with Tux, her dog. Life has dealt her a brutal and devasting card. She's right where she wants to be...alone.

But alone isn't necessarily what is good for her.

For all the
tears we've shed

For all the lovers, and all the tears we shed.

For all the Tears we've Shed

Dane

It was my first day starting work at a new school after the summer break. I knew it was going to be a grueling process, but I needed a change, and I needed it now. I was a teacher in a new school. I'd uprooted my kids to a fixer-upper house around the corner in a new town. My *wife* had left me when she was three months pregnant—with another man's baby and that was about as much as I knew about the situation. It was all I needed to know.

That was six months ago…

Today would be better, it had to be. It was seven in the morning, and I'd just dropped the girls at the new before school care center before getting into work extra early. I'd already been here the week before with my girls to set up the classroom during the break. I wanted it to feel like my own space, but I also wanted to be prepared to meet any nervous or antsy students who might be unsure of me. I was taking over a grade three class from a sweet lady who took early retirement to care for her elderly sister. Grade three sounded great in the Zoom interview. I'd decided to go easy on myself since I'd taught high school periodically over the years as a relief teacher when I was back on leave. If I was being honest, I needed a break from the attitudes of all those *'angry at the world'* teenagers. Grade three should be a breeze.

Mark came and knocked on my door with a hot coffee and an everything bagel just as I'd put my bag in my bottom drawer.

"Ready for this?" He smiled as he sipped his coffee while I opened the door.

I liked Mark, he was one year younger than me at 30 and I had been grateful for another male teacher in a female-dominated school. We had only met last week; he was the PE teacher and had been here since he graduated college, a native of Duluth.

"First day. How hard could it be?" I questioned.

"Don't be so sure, there's a lot of single moms around here, and they are hungry! I have to hide in my office during drop off and pick up times." Mark laughed.

Even in a tracksuit he was noticeably fit and kept himself clean-shaven and well groomed. He was slightly shorter than me, about six foot and he had dark blonde hair and hazel eyes.

I took a large gulp of the coffee and slumped in my seat and dumped my trench coat in a heap on the floor. I'll get a coat stand at some point or fix a hook to a wall I thought to myself.

"But maybe if they think I'm a slob…" I chuckled.

I was the epitome of slob, if any of them saw my house, they'd run for the hills. We were still living out of boxes, eating off of foldable camp tables, air mattresses and nor myself or the girls had eaten a meal that didn't come in paper or cardboard. The term slob was a kindness.

"Not likely, but good luck with that." He reached his hand out for a fist pump.

"Go and hide in your office. Thanks for breakfast." I grinned.

I placed math books on each desk and strung up a few lengths of fishing line over the roof to display the children's work.

Then there was another knock at the door.

"Hello?" said a young woman.

"Sorry, I can't let the kids in for another few minutes." I said as I looked at my watch avoiding eye contact a little annoyed that my prep time had been cut short.

"Oh, I'm not a parent. I'm your assistant for Mondays, I rotate between classes. They gave me to you cause apparently, we're both new here." She smiled.

Her eyes were light blue except for a brown patch in her left eye. My body relaxed to the warmth of her friendly nature, and I smiled instantly at the relief of having another adult around.

"I'm Dane." I leant in to shake her hand.

"Stella! Well, Estella, but just call me Stella." She said nervously as she held onto my hand a little too long while she seemed to map out my face.

"Estella, it's nice to make your acquaintance." I smiled as I retrieved my hand.

She couldn't have been too old. She was short, with brown hair and natural sun-bleached highlights tied back into a high ponytail like that singer something *Grande* and she was covered in what I assumed to be dog fur.

"Furry friend?" I asked as I offered her a lint roller from my desk.

"Oh no!" she looked down at her white shirt with tuffs of black hair.

I laughed a little to myself as she figured out the roller and finally peeled off a strip of used tape.

"My dog, Tuxedo. Well, Tux. He's a big black Newfoundland. He gives the best hugs, but everyone will know." she sighed as she swiped the roller over her chest.

"At least it wasn't drool." I added.

"Luckily for me, he's not a dribbly Newfoundland, which would be a disaster." She smiled.

"Can I put my bag somewhere?" her eyes latched onto me again as she stood upright handing me the roller.

"The bottom drawer is where I put my stuff, feel free to share it." I was pacing nervously now as parents and students began to fill the corridors and I was due to open the door soon.

"Ready?" I asked Stella as she straightened herself up.

She brushed herself off one final time and put on a layer of lip balm and gave me the nod to open the doors.

"Come in everyone." I greeted the parents and students.

The students and parents were already well acquainted and in their groups of gossipy moms, PTA moms, working moms panicking on their phones, helicopter moms, and the odd couple of married parents, all glaring at me waiting for me to say something intelligible. I stood back smiling unless a parent wished to approach me, but kept a warm demeanor about myself, hoping I looked friendly and approachable. Stella was much more involved and hands-on, she already had crayons out with two students and some younger siblings coloring as their parents gossiped between themselves often darting me racy looks.

I waved over one family and introduced myself. A married couple seemed like a good target.

"Hello, I'm Mr. De La Roche." I bent down and shook a little boy's hand, and he smiled before running off to his friends.

The volume in the room grew. The time was ticking by, and I knew soon the parents would leave. That's when the real task would begin.

"Good morning, everyone. Students and families. You can all call me Mr. De. I look forward to getting to know you all." I announced.

"Welcome to our community." One mom clapped, her smile so wide I could see her gums.

"We need more male teachers." Her friend grinned and I couldn't help but feel my stomach turn as I imagined Mark tucked away safely in his office.

Stella grinned with her head down in a coloring sheet with some younger siblings before she met my gaze and gave me a thumbs up, her cheeks rosy and the sides of her lips so wide they might almost touch her ears. She had no composure as she assessed the room of women gawking at me like a piece of meat and I slung my trench coat back on rather fast as I felt my shirt tighten every time I moved, hugging my tensed biceps.

"Well, if any parents ever want to discuss anything, my door is always open. I don't bite." I knew I fucked that up, and the hungry vixens in the front would cream themselves at the word *bite*.

So far, I could tell my classroom was a ratio of professional parents who knocked, kissed, and ran out the door, and then there were the school moms, the ones who made school their whole lives. The type who kept having kids just to come back here for something to do and read those pornographic books to numb reality once they were home. In-between were the introverts, the ones who were a little shy, and never said too much, but their kids' lunches looked like they came from a Michelin-star restaurant, I wanted them to make my lunches, I wanted anyone to make my lunch. I was a two-minute noodle guy and Cassie was always on my case about it.

The last six months I and the girls had survived on a diet of overcooked pasta, and soggy frozen pizzas which somehow, I'd burn the crust of. Lilly my youngest would hide under the bin bag hoping I wouldn't see them. She must have forgotten who emptied the bins in our house, but I never let on that I knew. Then there was the cereal, we had a whole shelf dedicated to cereal boxes. We had every kind possible and the girls made videos of themselves trying each one once a week and often ordered cereal in from other countries when we could afford it.

The day flew by, and it turned out that Cassie my second eldest daughter was in the classroom next door and Audrey my oldest was in the class one more door down from hers.

"Daddy?" Cassie knocked on the door.

"Come in Cassie." I said as I turned off my computer and squeezed her for a hug.

"Audrey's getting Lilly." She whispered; she was a little shy of Stella.

"This is Stella." I introduced Cassie to her.

"Nice to meet you, Cassie." Stella smiled warmly. She was visibly knackered and just waiting for me to release her as she wiped down the benches even though she knew we had cleaners.

"You can go if you like Stella, I'll lock up." I spoke.

"Thanks for having me today. See you next Monday." She waved at me and Cassie as she left the room.

"WOAH! Did you see her eyes?" Cassie gasped.

"Stella has heterochromia, it's when one of your eyes is a different color or partially different color." I explained.

"She's very beautiful." Cassie swooned as she spun in her skirt.

"Enough about Stella, how was your first day?" I sat her on the desk and gave her my full attention.

"Well, my teacher is nice. She said you're good looking and that's why I'm so pretty." She giggled as she flattened her hands under her chin. Her light brown hair was a knotty mess I dreaded brushing out later.

"I thought we tied this up?" I asked as I tugged gently at her locks.

"*You* did, but Heather said boys like girls with their hair down." Alarm bells went off when I heard boys.

"What boys? Who's Heather? She sounds awful." I gasped with a hint of laughter.

"Well, James is quite handsome." She fluttered her eyelashes, and I was grateful when Audrey stormed in with Lilly, cutting off Cassie from going further into her apparent crush on James.

"DADDY!" Lilly howled in tears.

"Oh, what's happened?" Audrey shrugged her shoulders and dumped her bag on a dcsk.

"I hate school!" she yelled.

"Why?" I asked.

"I'm tired." She replied.

"Aww Lillian. We are all tired, but it's your first day! What do you say we go home, order some Chinese, and watch a movie?" I asked.

In the corner of my eye, I could see Cassie threatening her as she mouthed the words '*Say yes!*' in Lilly's direction. Audrey's ears pricked up as she waited for the youngest member of our family to make the most important decision of our day.

"Okay." She leaped off the desk and skipped towards the door.

"Phew." Cassie sighed and her head comically dropped.

"That was a close one." I gave her a high-five.

If there's one thing we agreed on, it's that my cooking wasn't a good idea *ever*. I trusted Audrey to cook the two-minute noodles more than I trusted myself.

Cassie was eight and had mastered grilled cheese toasties as long as Audrey was making the tomato soup—from a can of course.

Audrey was ten, often in her own little world reading books and leaving a trail of mess behind her wherever she went, but she had a keen interest in cooking, so I bought her a bunch of Gordon Ramsay cookbooks. I had hoped she'd bury herself in *those* books and cook us fabulous meals, but she always complained I bought the wrong ingredients, so all aspirations there were short-lived since I apparently didn't know the difference between salted and unsalted butter.

Lilly was only five and the tension after the separation had impacted her the most. She was a mommy's girl and when Gina broke the news, I was even more shocked when she admitted she didn't want custody of the girls, not that I complained. But I was devastated for them, knowing she felt the way she did.

I didn't fight her on it, if she didn't want them in that moment then they wouldn't be loved or nurtured the way they deserved. She said she never felt right being a girl mom and now that she was having a boy, she wanted a fresh new start. *Bitch!* I could have said a million things, but the worst thing she could hear was silence as I opened the door behind her and nudged her out. She wept on the doorstep for a good hour as I sat on the other side with my face in my palms wondering how it got to this point.

Her boyfriend picked her up and punched and spat at the door and called me all sorts of names through the door in her defense. If the girls hadn't been in the house, I'd have gone out there and slapped him around, but I knew I had to be the bigger person now. So, I let him throw his tantrum and beat up his knuckles on my hardwood front door. To this day I still don't know his identity, nor have I laid eyes on him and that's how I wanted to keep it.

It was then and there I called our real estate agent and had the house put on the market. The girls and I were out two weeks later and road-tripping from the south to Minnesota.

The kids ate Uncrushables and Doritos the whole way and drank litres of Faygo. Something *we* had never let them do before. But it wasn't *we* anymore—it was *me.*

Things hadn't been good for about two years, but she did a damn good job of hiding her affair and I guess once they got pregnant, she was already so detached from our family it was an easy move for her.

"Order already!" Lilly's tummy grumbled.

"Okay, sheesh. Calm down." I laughed.

"I want egg rolls." Cassie announced.

"I'll have lemon chicken." Audrey added.

I dialed the local Chinese restaurant, and they picked up on the first ring. "What would you like to order?" an old lady asked in a thick accent.

"Can I order the egg rolls, lemon chicken, fried rice, chow mein, broccoli beef, wonton soup, fried dumplings, and some fortune cookies." I had to take a deep breath after that.

"Okay, see you in ten minutes." The old lady hung up without taking my details and we googled the directions to the store.

"That's fast." I hummed.

"Good, I'm starving." Audrey smiled.

"Yeah Dad, I can't keep living on PB&J Uncrustables. I got   in   trouble   today   because they aren't *approved*." Cassie groaned.

"Why is your teacher peeking into your lunchbox?" I grunted.

"She   says   she   supports   healthy   eating,   and I shouldn't have so much sugar in my lunch box.

I grumbled *'Well she can make your fucking lunches'* below my breathe. I hated making lunch and this was why. People would see it, and as a teacher I knew there'd be some nosey parker, parking her eyeballs in my kids' lunch bag—I was also guilty of this, but because their food looked better than mine, I wasn't judging any child who came to school with some sort of food, as long as they were eating.

"I think we'll open a cafeteria account." I sighed.

The girls cheered immediately.

"Oh my god! I'm so getting the cheeseburger tomorrow." Cassie whispered to Audrey.

"I'm getting the pizza! It won't be burnt *or* soggy." Lilly giggled.

"Hey! I don't complain about your cooking." I chuckled.

"I don't cook daddy." Lilly laughed.

"You pour milk on my cereal and last time it was too soggy. I'm making a formal complaint!" I joked.

"You're so silly." She smiled as we pulled up to the Chinese restaurant.

We all climbed out of the old jeep and a bell chimed as we entered the packed restaurant.

"Phone order?" an old lady asked.

"Ughh yes." I was stunned at the hustle and bustle.

She then followed by repeating our whole order and I was miffed as to how she knew who it belonged to me without taking any of my details.

"Sorcery!" Cassie wiggled her fingers at Lilly.

I swiped my credit card and grabbed the bags and placed them in the front seat as the girls climbed into the back seat.

"Strap that in, Dad! We don't want to lose the precious cargo." Audrey winked into the rearview mirror.

I nodded back into the mirror and secured the seatbelt around the food as ordered.

It was after five when we arrived home and Lilly as always stole my keys to unlock the front door, so she was the first one inside.

"First one in sets the table!" I yelled out.

"Grab her bag please girls." Audrey was already all over it as Cassie collected Lilly's shoes and socks. They held the door open for me while I brought in the food and Lilly was laying out paper plates and disposable wooden cutlery.

The smart, yet hardly conscious side of me had put the ceramic plates in cupboards too high for the girls to reach so they wouldn't be broken, but now we never use them.

Admittedly paper plates were my best friend. I hated dishes, so this was perfect.

"Good job Lil!" I patted her shoulder.

The girls helped themselves to their favorite dishes and I settled in with beef and broccoli.

"Can I have a little tree?" Cassie asked as she eyed my broccoli.

"You're so weird." Audrey teased.

Cassie already had her hands on my plate like a caveman as she stole three of my pieces of broccoli.

"You can pay me in an egg roll." I smiled.

"Here." She launched an egg roll onto my plate.

Lilly was already in the fortune cookie bag cracking them all open.

"Hey, save some for us." Audrey snatched the bag.

"What does yours say, Lil?" I asked.

"*What good are wings, without the courage to fly.*" She read aloud.

"Mine says '*If you want the rainbow, you gotta put up with the rain.*'" Said Cassie.

"And mine says '*All the effort you are making will ultimately pay off.*'" Audrey said as caught my eye and gave me a half smile and held my hand from across the table.

"What's yours say, Daddy?" Lilly asked.

"*Follow what calls you.*" I read.

"I like that one." Audrey said as she slurped some wonton soup.

"So do I." I agreed.

Cassie retrieved all of our fortunes and stuck them in the empty cookie jar on top of the fridge. We always saved our fortunes until the next time we had Chinese and replaced them. It was a weird tradition we had started when we found so many of them lying around the house. Instead of throwing them in the trash, the girls stuck them in a jar, and it brought us joy to reflect on them.

"Okay, showers!" I ordered as I packed away the leftover food and put the plates in the trash.

They marched into their barely sorted rooms and grumbled as they hunted for pajamas. I knew I fucked up. I hadn't done any washing in the time we had been here and as I entered the laundry room it was like a pink pile of death was staring at me. It was the height of Audrey now and I hadn't even hooked up the washing machine, but now we were running out of clean clothes.

"Fuck." I growled.

"DAD!" Cassie was behind me.

"And you were doing so well…" Audrey scolded as she reached to pat me on the back.

"That's one dollar in the jar." Lilly waved her index finger at me from left to right with her other arm under her elbow.

"Do me a favor, just find something else to wear to bed tonight while I go to war with this nightmare." I sighed as I pulled out a dollar for Lilly to add to the same jar that ironically housed our fortunes.

I plugged the washing machine into the wall and attached the hoses and turned it on.

"FUCK!" I yelled once more. I remembered I hadn't even bought laundry detergent.

I knelt on the floor and pulled out another Washington and held the dollar above my head as I heard Lilly's footsteps beelining for the laundry room as if my profanities summoned her chipper presence.

"Thank you!" She chuckled as she unfolded the bill and held it up to the light with a squint.

But she noticed my defeat. On my knees, we were at eye level and her cheeky grin softened into pity.

"You're doing a good job, Daddy." She hugged me and gave me a pat on the back.

"Thank you, baby. I'm trying." I sighed into her hair that smelt of a classroom, the sweaty kind.

"Dad, we have no towels left." Cassie exclaimed as she dropped a pile of musky damp dirty towels in the doorway.

"Everyone in the car." I grunted.

"Where are we going?" Lilly beamed.

"Costco." I replied.

The girls didn't protest. They knew they'd likely get dessert, so they did as they were told and communicate this knowledge with wide eyes glares at one another and pursed lips.

We pulled up to Costco and Audrey grabbed a cart.

"Towels and detergent only, it's late." I tried to be firm.

"Well, you should probably buy us some pajamas." Lilly grinned and Audrey nodded to agree.

They were right, and while I was here it was probably worth stocking up on everything we really needed—We needed a lot.

I grabbed four towels to get us through the night, a set of pajamas each, laundry detergent, unstoppables, a bunch of cereal to add to the shelf, some boxes of instant ramen, milk, frozen dumplings, chicken wings, and some snacks for school.

"We're done." I announced as the girls began scanning the board for the ice cream at the cafeteria.

"I want the strawberry sundae." Lilly tugged at me.

"Chocolate, we'll share." Cassie and Audrey said in unison.

I went to the counter and placed the order as the girls took a seat on the red benches.

"Here we go." I handed out spoons and let Lilly have first dibs on the strawberry sundae.

"Thanks, Dad!" the girls chimed.

I looked around the food court, it was full of mostly workers on their breaks, one other family, and a few couples and then I saw Stella. I recognized her clothes and her ponytail. She was alone and had no cart but was eating a hotdog and had a whole roast chicken on the table in front of her.

"Dane?" She covered her mouth as she swallowed her food, a little tomato sauce on her bottom lip.

I shook a napkin in her direction, and she walked over, took the napkin politely, and wiped her face.

"Oh, Stella!" Cassie smiled.

"Hi Cassie, funny seeing you here." Stella had a gentle nature and was great with kids and I dreaded the day without her tomorrow.

"Doing some shopping?" I attempted small talk as Cassie patted the bench beside her for Stella to join us, she obliged and took a seat.

"Actually, I just came for a quick dinner. And I got another one for my dog, Tux." She smiled. She was covered in dog fur again and she held up the extra hotdog and chicken.

"These are my sisters, Lilly and Audrey." Cassie introduced them as Lilly, and I fought with our spoons for the most sauce.

"How was your first day?" I asked.

"It was great, I'm exhausted though, ready for a hot shower and a good sleep." She snickered as she handed me a clean napkin to wipe the strawberry sauce from my chin that Lilly had painted on me.

"Whose class are you in tomorrow?" I questioned.

"I think Mrs. Lambert." She answered.

"That's my teacher!" exclaimed Audrey.

"Oh good! I'll have one familiar face." She smiled at Audrey.

"How old are you?" Audrey asked.

"I'm twenty-six." She answered.

"Do you live here?" Lilly asked.

"Kind of…" She answered a little puzzled.

"Huh?" Lilly was confused.

"I live in my van. It's a house on wheels and I travel around to different places. I decided I liked Duluth a lot when I stopped here a month ago so I found a job so I could stay a little while." She explained.

Lilly was invested and made it very obvious Stella was now her idol, she always wanted to play in the car, and to hear that Stella lived in her car would have shot her to stardom in her eyes.

"Can we see it?" Cassie begged.

"If your dad says it's okay." She nodded as she looked to me for approval.

"Well, rubbish in the trash." I stood up eager to get home to tackle that mound of dirty laundry.

We followed Stella out to the parking lot. She was parked two cars away from us. She pulled the sliding door open and Tux, a big fluffy Newfoundland demanded her attention and sniffed around for his treat.

"You have a bear!" Lilly squealed and jumped behind me.

"Oh, he's a   dog. Don't worry Lilly,   Tux   is   very gentle." She took him outside and let the girls pat him.

The girls swooned over him. Tux was quick to lick any residue of ice cream from their faces.

The van was quite tidy, nothing like our house. It had a small bathroom and toilet, a one-burner stove, a tiny sink, a small fridge, and a bed that looked like a cloud. From what I could tell, I was being nosey.

"I didn't skimp on my beauty sleep." She caught me examining her home.

"I wouldn't have either." I smiled curiously.

"Where do you do your washing?" Cassie asked.

"I go to a laundromat." She answered.

"Oh, we haven't done any washing." She outed me.

"That's the whole reason we're here." She added with a cheeky giggle.

"Well, you just moved here, right? I'm sure Dad's been busy." She gave me a forgiving wink.

"Yeah, he's trying." Audrey came to my defense and Tux put his paw on my leg as I patted his soft long fur.

"Why don't we hire a nanny? Heather has a nanny, and she does all their housework." Cassie questioned.

"Nannies are a little expensive." I sighed.

"Dad's right girls, they aren't cheap. I'm sure he's got a handle on things." She gave me a gentle nudge in the rib to make me agree.

"If we get out of here, it's almost bedtime and you all still stink!" I teased.

"Goodnight girls, see you at school." Stella waved as we walked towards our car.

She had Tux in front of her and held his paw to wave goodbye.

We finally arrived home, and the girls skipped off to the shower with their clean clothes and towels while I put away all the shopping.

I was staring down the pile of washing once again when the girls all appeared with brushed wet hair in their new winter pajamas.

"Much better." I smiled.

"Goodnight Daddy, tonight was fun! Can we see Tux again?" Cassie asked.

"You'll have to ask Stella." I shrugged.

"I have her tomorrow, I'll ask!" Audrey said.

"Okay, off to bed ladies." I walked them each into their rooms.

The house had four bedrooms and the girls had demanded their own rooms. The upstairs level was a large open space with its own bathroom. Once I'd fixed up the paint job and replaced the windows, I was going to use it as office space and somewhere to put the girl's excessive number of toys and all of Audrey's books.

Once I'd kissed the girl's goodnight I went back to the laundry and rubbed my eyes as I attempted to separate the whites from all the pink and ran a load of towels in the meantime.

In the living room was a tornado of even more dirty clothes, Lilly's dolls, Audrey's books, the new damp towels hung over the suede couch, and school bags were tossed randomly in different corners with stinky lunchboxes still with half-eaten apples and bananas.

The house had no order, and I had no time. Cassie was right. We needed a nanny, or someone to help somehow.

The grass in the yard was too long for the girls to play in and the pool would soon be frozen over once winter rolled in.

I needed help, I couldn't keep feeding us all junk food and take-out. I was never going to get used to all the washing, drying, folding, and packing away.

What I really needed was a beer and a blowjob. At least I could have one of those. It was the only other thing in our fridge before the Costco trip other than Uncrushables and the almost expired milk.

Stella

Poor Dane, his bags had bags and I could see he was trying so hard. He had been great to work with and he wasn't bad to look at, tall with green eyes, dark brown hair with a few silver strands, and a muscular build that he hid poorly under his professional sweater. The kind of guy who didn't know how hot he was. He was so busy being a dad he had forgotten himself. Lucky for his wife; hot husband, and three really sweet kids.

"C'mon Tux." I pulled out his bed from under the front seat as I blacked out all the windows so I could take my shower in the Walmart parking lot. Walmart was always the safest, they had CCTV.

The school was great, it was my first time working as a teacher's aide and it was only three days a week. I didn't need a lot of money without rent, but my contract was for twelve months, and I considered leasing a small apartment, so Tux had a bigger space to relax while I worked. I checked in on him every break I had, left the roof windows open, and walked him during my lunch break, but he deserved more space to himself. Most nights I caved anyway and let him in the bed with me which made my white linen look more like storm clouds.

The next morning was windy as fall truly began to take over and the last few sunny days would soon be behind us. I woke up at six and stretched before I made my morning coffee and washed my face. I pulled on some black pants and a black shirt paired with a comfy, but acceptable sweater and a pair of sneakers. My hair I brushed into a ponytail, and I added a coat of mascara to help me look slightly more alive.

I drove to school a little while later and Tux nudged at me as he recognized the parking lot.

"I'm sorry boy. This is how I feed us." I sighed as I hugged him tight.

A knock at my window scared me and I screamed while Tux barked and raced for the door. It was Dane, he had recognized my van. I opened the door and Tux paced around him excitedly.

"Sorry, I didn't mean to scare you." He apologized.

"I just wanted to tell you the girls might ambush you for a play date with your fur child." He leaned down to Tux and gave him pats and cuddles.

"He would love that! He's not a fan of me spending my days here." I sighed.

"Bored?" Dane asked as he looked up to the open windows and smiled in approval.

"I guess so, I come out when I can and walk him but it's not enough, the hours are long." I said as I rested my hands on my hips.

"Parenting isn't always easy." He agreed.

"No matter the species." I nodded.

"We have a big yard; it needs some work, but he could hang out there once I have the grass under control." Dane offered.

"Your wife wouldn't think it's weird she's babysitting some random girl's dog?" I laughed.

Dane forced a laugh "There is so no wife." He followed with an awkward cough to cover up his lack of interest in the topic.

"Oh, I'm sorry, I didn't mean to pry…" I cut myself off and started fidgeting with my hands.

"It's okay, you didn't know. Anyway, that means it's my decision whose dogs come play in my yard." He smiled.

When he smiled like that, *I* wanted the invitation to play in his yard, as long as his yard contained a mattress and some lubricant. *Stop that, Stella!* I scolded myself.

He seemed less nervous today. He was dressed well, just as he was yesterday. Today he wore the trench coat that was dumped on the floor with brown pants and darker brown leather shoes. His beard was a little scruffier and I liked how it made him a little darker and edgy.

"Stella?" He waved his hand in front of me as I looked through him.

"Sorry, I was thinking." I apologized.

"About the yard?" he asked.

"Yeah, definitely about the yard." I cleared my throat.

"Umm, I'd love that, I could pay you! And I'll help clean it up." I smiled.

"You don't need to pay me." Dane laughed. "You could do some washing.' He joked half-heartedly.

I smiled as I considered it with no time at all and before I knew what I was saying I nodded and accepted what I imagined to be a pyramid of dirty clothes.

"Yes, I only work three days, so I don't mind coming and helping if you're serious about doing this for me. Cassie did say you needed a little help." I said softly.

"A little is an understatement." He croaked.

"You're welcome to park in our front yard and use the water and electricity if you're truly willing to do housework. If I'm being honest, I feel like I'm drowning in it." His voice became shaky and nervous.

"You have no idea how much that would help me. I'm kinda tired of Walmart's parking lots." I confessed.

"A win for both of us! Okay, that's settled then. You'll move onto my front lawn and your dog will have boundless freedom and a gated pool in the summer in exchange for you doing our laundry." He chuckled.

"I'll take that offer!" I laughed as I reached out my hand to shake on the agreement.

"We live two streets over, number thirty-four." He took my hand and placed his other hand on Tux's paw.

He was warm and he seemed elated to have offloaded the laundry duties. I wasn't worried. Laundry for kids wasn't hard. Their clothes were small, and you only had to change their sheets once a week. I hope he didn't expect me to iron.

"Dane, I don't iron." I confessed as I moved my thumb over his hand and grinned a little.

"Neither do I." he winked.

"Phew." We released each other from our handshake grasp and sat on the step of my van while Tux sniffed around his car.

"What days are you free?" he asked.

"Thursday and Friday." I answered.

"Give me your phone." He asked and I handed it over to him.

He began typing his phone number into my phone and texted me the whole address.

"Come set yourself up after school today, we can connect the water and power." He smiled.

"I can't tell you how much I appreciate this." I beamed.

"Glad I can help and be helped." He laughed.

"I wish you were back in my class today." He grumbled. "I'm a little nervous to be alone around some of those parents." He confessed.

"Oh, yeah. I heard some of the chatter, you're a hot commodity!" I teased.

"I'd rather do my job without the thirsty mothers." He laughed.

"Sorry, I can't protect you today. You're on your own." I elbowed him softly.

"Even Mark hides in his office." He whispered.

"I heard Mr. Douglas does too and he's pushing fifty." I snickered playfully.

"I guess it's just a little something to entertain their days, all in good fun." He sighed.

"Absolutely, how often do you hear about teachers dating parents? The school board would have their heads." I snickered.

"Exactly." He nodded.

I twiddled my thumbs as an awkward silence lingered while we struggled to find something to talk about.

"Have you made many friends here?" he asked.

"Not really, there's people I make small talk with, but nobody I'd call if I had a flat tire." I laughed. "What about you?" I added.

"Ugh, I like Mark. He seems like a good guy. We only really just got here though, and I haven't even done a full grocery shop. The girls made me pack their cereal box collection. That's as organized as I get." He smiled at the thought of it.

"Cereal collection? Are the boxes full?" I was curious and this got my attention.

"Yeah, when we find a new cereal, we buy a box and shelve it. The girls make a video trying a new one every week on their YouTube channel and through the rest of the week we'll eat the whole box... if it's worthy." He explained. "I've spent a lot of nights eating cereal they didn't like for dinner." He laughed.

His laugh was infectious and his barely there wrinkles appeared a little more obvious when he laughed.

"That sounds like a very dad thing to do." I smiled. "What a cool idea!" I remarked.

"Do they have many subscribers?" I asked.

"Nearly ten thousand actually, it's pretty cool." You could tell he was proud of them.

"If they want one more, I'll subscribe." I smiled. I was curious about these videos, but I was also shopping for a new cereal, maybe they'd give me some good ideas.

"It's called '*WhySoCereal*'." He seemed embarrassed as he told me the name.

"You definitely came up with that…Batman guy?" I asked.

"You know it. You?" he asked.

"I'm more of a Thor girl." I admitted.

"Argh, she likes the muscles." He teased.

"When the time comes to choose, I would favor a man who could carry me out of a burning building effortlessly." I threw up my hands in defeat.

"Hence the ginormous dog?" he said as he stroked Tux.

"Tux is an excellent swimmer and I kayak often. He comes with me." I explained.

"He doesn't sink you?" he laughed.

"Newfoundland's are water dogs; he'll save me if we sink. See, I got it all planned out." I grinned.

"Is that so?" He held my gaze and his eyes brightened.

"I think I do…" My stomach did cartwheels when he did that intimate staring stuff.

"We better get in there." Dane stood up as he saw the administration staff arriving. "If I don't see you, I'll catch you at home." He winked as he walked off to give me space to get Tux sorted.

It was a cold day, but my skin ran warm at the smallest ounce of flirtation, and I gave myself a pep talk before I made any mistakes. *No relationships at work, it's bad news!*

"Bye Tux, I'll see you real soon." I kissed his head as he slumped onto his pullout bed and grunted.

I waved good morning to the staff in the office and checked my roster in the staff room that was tapped to the notice board.

Mrs. Lambert's class, Audrey's teacher. She hadn't let off anything about her class or teacher the way Cassie had. I walked down the hallway past the cafeteria and down a second corridor where I found Mrs. Lambert in her classroom writing on a whiteboard.

I knocked gently as I opened the door.

"Hi!" I smiled as I walked towards her.

"You must be Stella." She smiled back at me. "Glad to have you, these kids are older, somewhat rowdy and I'm getting too old to reel them in." she explained.

"Happy to help where I can." I assured her.

The bell rang and the students flooded into their classrooms. Audrey met my gaze and gave me a kind nod as she sat beside her friends and pulled out her books.

The day went faster than yesterday, the older kids were a little louder but also seasoned enough to follow instructions a little faster than grade three students.

Once the day was finally over, I rushed to my van and was greeted with my fluffy Tux and wrapped him in cuddles and spoiled him with his favorite jerky treat to show him how grateful I was that he hadn't made a mess or torn my bed into shreds.

"I love you, big guy!" I squeezed one more hug from him.

Dane and his girls appeared behind me, and they all appeared ecstatic as I smiled at them.

"You're moving in with us!" Lilly exploded.

I laughed out loud and sat on my step and Tux demanded her attention. "Not quite, I'll be a whole front lawn away from you though and when I'm at school Tux can hang out in your yard." I explained.

"Let's go." Dane showed the girls towards his car and motioned for me to follow him.

I climbed into the driver's seat and Tux jumped onto the passenger seat and he watched as I followed Dane two whole streets over like he had said. Tux was eager as he saw the girls waving from the rear window and he excitedly placed his paws on the dashboard.

We arrived moments later at a big house with a huge front yard, two large oak trees in the front with a treehouse sitting atop its strong expansive branches that together created the perfect nook to park my van. The house had a tall old white fence, a double garage, two stories with an attic, and a yellow marigold border weaved with the pathway to the front porch.

"This is stunning." I smiled at Tux who was dirtying my window with his tongue as Lilly jumped up and down excitedly for me to let him out.

I opened the door and stepped down after Tux. Dane was closing the gates before Tux could think to dash into the road.

"You can park beneath those trees." Dane said as he walked over to me.

"This place is beautiful." I swooned.

"It needs some work inside, probably why I got it at such a good price." He confessed.

"Put me to work." I smiled. "You're doing me a huge favor, I'm happy to help with any and all of it." I added.

"You good with tools?" Dane questioned, his brow a little furrowed as he considered my offer.

"I converted my whole van alone; I can find my way around a toolbox." I winked.

Dane smiled as he looked over at my van and then focused on me. "Okay, well first let me go mow the backyard quickly. Feel free to come inside and familiarize yourself with the place." He said as he began to walk down the side of the house to a shed.

"Girls, bring Tux inside." Dane shouted.

"Come on Stella! I want to show you, my room, even if it's empty." Cassie cooed.

I followed Cassie inside. Audrey and Lilly already had Tux on the couch and were brushing him with their hairbrushes and he was loving all the attention.

I could see Dane from the back doors mowing the lawn. He had taken off his work shirt and was pushing the mower in a singlet, his dress pants, and gum boots. I was right, his arms were thick, not too defined but they were hard-working arms, he had a naturally athletic physique, and I quivered a little when he caught me looking at him.

Cassie grasped my hand and pulled me in the direction of her room.

"It's nothing special yet, but I was thinking of a princess bed with those curtains that hang from the roof and something over the window…" she paused to think as she slumped onto the bed with her arms behind her head still daydreaming of the perfect girly bedroom.

"I love that idea! I think we could do so much with this room, it's huge!" I smiled. "I'm taking notes already." I winked as I tapped my temple.

"Really! Daddy says he doesn't have time for it." She sighed.

"Ugh, but that's why I'm here, so your dad has more time to do things with you all." I sat on the bed beside her.

"Thank you." She wrapped her arms around me and squeezed. I wrapped my arms around her and squeezed back gently.

"Speaking of helping your dad, can you point me to the laundry? I might get a head start." I winked at her, and she smiled as she pulled me down the hallway into a large laundry room with a washer and dryer and racks that came down from the walls that were full of freshly dried clothes.

"Woah. He wasn't joking." I laughed as I stood next to the pile comparing my height to it with my hand.

Audrey and Lilly came in and giggled aloud, and I made myself comfortable on the floor sorting the damp towels from the clothes and they suddenly sighed at the sight of the room.

"We'll help you!" Audrey sat beside me.

"Okay, Lilly. You find all the white things. Audrey, you can find all the socks, I have some washing bags in my van we can stick them in, so they don't get lost in the wash. Cassie, you can pull all those clothes down and place them in an empty basket." The girls agreed and got stuck into their assigned jobs.

"Back in just a minute, I'll go get those bags for the socks." I jumped up and quickly ran outside.

Dane was in the front yard now and his singlet was tucked into the back of his pants and my body almost gave way as I peeked a glance at his chest. *He's your boss, stop perving!* I growled to myself.

I stepped up into the van, pulled out my two laundry bags, and raced across the grass avoiding eye contact with any part of Dane's body.

"Okay, I have them!" I exclaimed as I entered the laundry.

"Cassie and Lilly got bored, so they left, but I'll help." Said Audrey.

"Aww, that's okay. You don't have to unless you want to." I smiled.

"It would be good for me to learn though right? And Dad's not the best at this." She laughed.

I grinned widely as she confessed her lack of faith in Dane's washing abilities. I picked up the basket with four towels and walked it over to the machine as Audrey followed me.

"Maybe a few more towels but we just add a tide pod, a little shake of unstoppables, and one cap of softener. Then we press this button and adjust the water temperature to hot, warm, or cold." She took mental notes and pulled at the pile as she hunted for some more towels to add to the drum.

"Can I press start?" she asked.

"Of course!" I watched her close the lid, adjust the water temperature, and press start.

"Oh, is this a normal load?" she pondered over the next option.

"Let's go with heavy-duty, just to be safe." I nodded.

"I might go shower now." She smiled at herself with pride as she wandered off to the bathroom.

I wandered through the kitchen, curious to find the cereal shelf. There was a large, long shelf stretched across the top of the fridge and it seemed to be the only thing in the house that was organized; each cereal was organized by expiration date.

There were moving boxes everywhere, the kitchen was barely unpacked, and the drawers had only disposable utensils in them. A large plastic bag on the bench beside the unused stove had paper plates and the overflowing rubbish bag was full of crushed pizza boxes and Chinese takeout.

I peered into the fridge that had only eggs, milk, and cheese. On the countertop was half a loaf of bread. *These guys can't eat takeout again tonight…*I cringed inside.

On a whim, I raced back out to my van and pulled out the large pack of chicken breasts Tux and I had been chipping away at, a jar of Italian sauce, flour, and some olive oil.

Once I was back inside, I had to improvise. I unpacked a box marked, pans and chopping boards. Inside was a brand-new chopping block, some knives, and a large pan.

I used the large knife to butterfly the chicken breasts, the back of the pan was all I had to tenderize them before I dredged them in flour, then egg wash and the old loaf of bread I shredded as best I could with my hands to create breadcrumbs.

 My fingers were thick and sticky when the girls came out clean and washed in pajamas as Audrey combed through Lilly's hair and she tried to run away.

"OH MY GOD… you cook??" Cassie squealed.

"Sure, want to help?" Secretly I was hoping she would manifest potatoes and maybe even peel them for me.

"No, but can we watch?" She sat on a stool on the bench and her sisters soon followed once Audrey had combed through the rest of Lilly's hair.

"Of course." I agreed.

"I'm just about to fry off the chicken schnitzels which I'll then turn into chicken parmigiana." I explained. "Does everyone like that?" I froze as I waited for replies.

"What is it?" Lilly asked.

"It's like a big chicken nugget with tomato sauce and cheese." Audrey explained.

"YES!" Lilly replied as she hunched over the counter anxiously.

"Do you guys have potatoes?" I asked with some worry.

I looked between them all as they shrugged together. The back door was open, and the sea of grass had disappeared, Tux was outside sniffing around an overgrown veggie patch, and to the left was an empty pool.

"That's okay." I smiled.

I turned back to the stove and flipped some of the chicken while the girls watched some YouTube videos. Ten minutes later Dane appeared beside me, still shirtless and smelling like freshly cut grass with an arm full of potatoes and a head of over-ripe lettuce.

"Do you think you can salvage this?" Dane handed me the lettuce.

I looked up at him realizing he had overheard me and the girls talking. "I'll do my best. He stood before me with the potatoes still in his arms and I began to pluck them out and place them in the sink to the side of us. He could have easily dropped them all in there, but I felt a heat between us, and the way he looked at me, he felt it too. *STELLA!* I groaned unwillingly in my head.

"What abundance." I smiled.

"The veggie garden is full, girls why don't we get out of Stella's hair and go pick some veggies?" he suggested.

"Ugh no thanks, I just showered." Audrey yawned.

"Ditto, I can't get dirt on these, the last pair remember." Cassie teased.

"Well, never mind then, I'll go alone." He sighed.

"Wait, I'm almost done frying these. Give me five minutes while I top them. If you like you can figure out how to turn the broiler on?" I slightly begged, only slightly.

He nodded and bent down trying to understand the nozzles that had no markings from the wear and tear of the older house.

Minutes passed and I had finished topping the chicken just in time for Dane to be done lighting the broiler. He set the temperature to medium-low and took the tray from me and placed it under the broiler.

"Let's go find a salad." He pulled himself up.

Dane

I followed her as she led the way outside and she looked around for the veggie garden.

"Just there." I pointed. "It was hidden behind all of that long grass."

"What a score!" she said as she began walking towards it.

As we walked, I felt her anxiousness. The way her eyes avoided me.

"I hope it's okay that I cooked. I had a bunch of chicken that was taking up too much space anyway and I'll replace the bread, milk, and cheese. I'm really sorry if I overstepped. I did some washing too." She started talking too fast as she apologized and her face became red and flushed with anxiousness.

I paused and grabbed her arm. "Don't apologize, I appreciate everything. The girls are even showered. They never shower when I ask them to." He laughed.

"They did that on their own." She explained.

"Well, that's a new development." He grinned.

"Regardless, I'll try to be more mindful and not get in your space when I don't need to be here." She finally caught my eye through the vines of tomatoes, each of us on one side.

"You can be here as much as you like, and you don't need to replace anything. I just need to do grocery shopping." I laughed trying to lighten the mood.

I pulled more vegetables from the garden and filled my arms as best I could. Stella had begun to use her shirt as a hammock for all the produce she couldn't carry and it revealed her honey-kissed skin, her belly button just in sight. Her hair draped around her face as she brushed it away with her dirty fingers and she left a smudge on her cheek.

"I should go and check on the chicken." She said as she waited for me to join her.

"Come here." I ordered. She froze though and I moved closer to her. I pulled my shirt off the back of my pants and wiped the dirt from her cheek. Her mouth fell open, and a heavy breath escaped her.

She looked up at me, pulled the shirt from my hands, and reached up to wipe the cold sweat and dirt off my face. It was wildly intimate and sexy, but she wasn't here for me, not like that.

She pulled away before I could, and we walked back to the house in silence.

"Oh no, I don't have a mitten." She exclaimed as she rushed to shut off the broiler.

"Here." I grabbed the tray out with the same shirt I still had in my hand. "They look perfect." I inhaled the smell of them.

"Go shower, I'll throw some sides together." She shooed me away playfully with her hands.

I stepped into the bathroom and the smell of her cooking wafted all through the house and it felt a little more like home. The girls' towels were tossed on the floor, but I was surprised to see they had at least kept their clothes in one pile altogether. I stood in front of the mirror as I ruffled grass out of my hair and took off my clothes.

The shower ran hot almost instantly, and I felt more at ease. Maybe it was the extra help, the company, and an adult to talk to, but today felt lighter. Most days I was wearing a mask just to get from seven am to five pm. Home life hadn't been much better, the girls rebelled in a unified manner. Objecting to showers, and sneaking junk food into their rooms. Most of the time they were great, but there was always fighting, they were growing up fast and it was unfamiliar territory for me since I spent so much time away from home in the past.

Stella hadn't wasted a second. She was practically a stranger to us, yet so willing to help and had no trouble getting the girls to like her, or my students. It just came effortlessly to her; she was just a likable person.

She was so young and beautiful. She must have thought I was such a creep touching her face. I was too old for her; I had no business even thinking about her. But here I was in the shower rock hard over the woman who just cooked me and my daughter's dinner.

It took me a few minutes to relieve myself and finally, I could wrap up my shower just as a knock fell on the door.

"Dane." It was Stella.

"Do you have a clean towel?" She asked.

Shit, of course, I didn't. I usually just sprinted down the hall naked since I never showered when the girls were awake.

"No." I replied.

"I'm coming in, my eyes are closed." She walked through the piles of clothes on the floor and stood with a towel in her arms.

I shut the water off and took the towel from her.

"Thank you." I said graciously.

"It's still warm." I hugged it to my chest.

"Fresh out of the dryer." Her eyes were still squeezed shut. "Okay, I'm going to finish dinner." She escaped from the bathroom just in time.

I could have taken her here on the floor on all the damp towels and mats after that. She was hot and thoughtful…and she was cooking me dinner. *Not just you asshole, your kids too.* My inner monologue was alive, awake, and enjoying every ounce of this self-torture I had invited into my home.

I wrapped the towel around my pelvis and walked to my room where I dressed in a grey shirt and flannelette pants. The smells were overwhelming me now, garlic from the garden and onions floated through the air.

"That smells divine." I expressed as I walked into the kitchen where Stella was crying over dicing more onions.

"Let me do that." I moved her out of the way, and she raced to wash her hands and face under the tap. Tux looked worried but he smelt the food and licked his lips as he waited patiently to be fed.

"Don't worry, you get a bowl too buddy." I assured him.

"Here, put those in this bag to freeze." She ordered as she handed me a zip-lock bag.

"Huh?" I asked.

"You'll never use all of those before they go bad, I'm going to freeze them for you." She pointed to a big dirty pile of onions in the sink. Tears began to flow from my own eyes. The rest of the kitchen was clean already and dishes she had used were drying on a tea towel.

"Dinner's ready, you can stop for now." She wiped her face with a paper towel. I pulled the paper towel from her hands once she was done and wiped the tears from my face.

"Thank god!" I smiled.

We took a seat at the table with the girls who already had the plates and cutlery set out.

"I'm very impressed girls, I didn't have to ask you to do a single thing tonight. Thank you." I smiled at them all.

They seemed chuffed with themselves, and they smiled back. Stella served them each a parmigiana and asked if they wanted any salad or garlic potatoes. None for Lilly or Audrey but Cassie was interested in the potatoes. She tried the potatoes first and politely asked for more after her first bite.

"Okay, give me some of those before Cassie eats them all." I joked as I held out my hand for the tray.

Stella handed me the tray and served herself a plate of food but got up to feed Tux outside before she settled to eat.

"This is delicious!" Lilly said with sauce all over her face.

"I'm so glad you like it; I don't think I've ever cooked for kids." Stella replied.

"You're a natural." Audrey winked as she plucked a potato from Cassie's plate.

Stella blushed as she ate her food, the girls never took their eyes off her, they were just as impressed as I was.

"It really is good, thanks Stella. You can cook for us anytime you like." I smiled from across the table.

"Thank you." Her smile softened as her eyes caught mine and she seemed tired.

The beeper on the washer went off and she sprung up to go and check it.

"I like her." Audrey whispered to us all.

"She's really pretty too." Lilly added.

"Best idea ever, Dad!" Cassie winked.

I was proud but also freaking out. I had to keep my distance if I wanted to avoid fucking this up. I hadn't had sex in years. Gina had made sure of that long before we separated. I wasn't the cheating type regardless of how poorly she had been. Subconsciously I had known for years she was being unfaithful, I just never wanted to break up the family we had. She did that all on her own.

"Okay, another ten loads and we should be on track." Stella joked as she slumped down to eat. "Good news, the towels are all done." She fist-pumped Audrey.

"We did it!" Audrey cheered.

And now she had my oldest learning how to do washing, was she a sorceress…

We all finished our food, and I went around with a bin bag to collect all the rubbish.

"Thanks for being such great hosts! I better get back to my van and shower…and sleep." She smiled as she stood up to yawn.

"Do you want to shower here?" I asked.

"Tempting, but I don't have any shoes that I can sprint across freshly cut grass in that'll keep me clean." She said.

"Stay here tonight, I'll take the couch." What was I saying, I hated sleeping on the couch.

"I don't want to keep putting you out, Dane." She sighed as if she were guilty for it all.

"Don't do that, don't feel bad, you're helping me more than I'm helping you. You're welcome to my bed anytime you want it." Fuck, what did I just say?

She grinned as she tried not to laugh at me. "I know what you meant." She recoiled.

"I unplugged the hose to mow the lawns, I'll reconnect it now if you want. No pressure to stay here." I assured her.

"Okay, you twisted my arm. I'll stay the night. I just need to get some clothes." She walked out the front door and I sprinted to my room to tidy it. An impossible task, there were boxes everywhere.

"Daddy, can we watch a movie?" Audrey came and asked.

"Sure, go put something on, I just have to tidy up for Stella." I nodded.

I stripped the bed of the bed sheets and the pillows. A box labeled bed stuff in Cassie's handwriting sat in the corner and I pulled it open searching for a king-size fitted sheet and pillowcases.

"Dane." Stella's voice was behind me.

"Hey! Just changing the smelly man sheets for you." I felt embarrassed she had caught me.

"You shouldn't have." She came over to help me, dumping her bag full of clothes in the corner of my room.

She was so much better at putting fitted sheets on than I was and so I retreated to the pillowcases before she could notice how poorly domesticated, I was.

"Okay, done." She fluffed the duvet and sprawled it over the bed.

I hurled the pillows onto the bed, and I desperately wanted to dive into it…with her. *Off limits!* There was that voice again. Stella began unpacking her pajamas. A grey shirt like mine and pink shorts. My heart sang when she didn't pull out underwear. Maybe she went commando just like me.

"Let me clear out that mess before you go in there." I sighed.

"I'm making more work for you." She bit her bottom lip.

"NO, you're worth it. I mean, you've done enough for me in one day already." I corrected myself.

I raced to the bathroom before she could look at me and I picked up the clothes the girls had left on the floor and took them to the laundry. I was thrilled when I noticed the pile of washing had decreased by almost half and the towels were all folded and tucked away in a cupboard, the air-drying rack had been folded and put away. Something I didn't know how to do. The washer was washing a load of what looked like to be my clothes and there were three baskets of steaming hot clothes waiting to be folded.

Stella came in and grabbed a basket of the girls' clothes and brought it into my room.

"Hey, go and take a shower!" I ordered.

"Just a second, I'm going to fold these once I'm done, I'll shower." She said.

"Can't it wait?" I asked.

"The girls need clothes for tomorrow." She replied.

I nodded and agreed, but I was feeling pretty guilty that she had worked all day and was now spending all her time off caring for us.

"I'll help." I went back to the laundry room and piled the last two baskets on top of each other and brought them down to my room. I tried to act like I knew what I was doing.

I had successfully sorted socks from the giant pile and Stella finally gave up and retreated to shower. She appeared a few minutes later in her pajamas, freshly washed hair and smelling like bubblegum. I hadn't seen her with her hair down before, it sprawled across her back in a wavy heap.

"You're doing well." She joked.

"Laundry isn't my strength." I sighed.

"You did warn me." she laughed. "But really, I don't mind. Go spend some time with your kids." She was genuine and sweet.

"You sure? We don't have to tackle all of this now. You can come watch the movie if you like?" I offered.

"That does sound tempting. What are we watching?" She asked.

"I think I heard Audrey say Homeward Bound." I replied.

"That's Tux's favorite! Count me in." She beamed.

We walked to the lounge room where the girls already had their pillows and blankets on the couch and a mattress had been dragged out and sat on the floor in front of the TV. Tux was nestled cozily across all three of the girls with his eyes watching eagerly for the movie to start.

"Where are we going to sit?" I scuffed Lilly's hair.

"That's why we pulled the mattress out. You guys can lay on the floor since you always fall asleep during movies Daddy." Audrey snickered.

"Are they allowed popcorn?" Stella whispered.

"We don't have any." I whispered back.

"There's some in my van." She said.

"Do you want me to go get it?" I asked.

"If you like, it's just in the second drawer to the left of the fridge." She smiled. "Microwave it in there, yours isn't too reliable."

"Yeah, I hate it already." I laughed as I headed out to the van.

I hadn't been in a van like this before. It was cozy and had only the essentials. A small sink, one burner, a mini bathroom with a toilet inside and of course a big bed. I rummaged through the drawer she had mentioned and found two packets of microwave popcorn and stuck one in the microwave. As I waited curiosity got the best of me and I went through a few cupboards, mostly food, Tux's food, bathroom stuff, and laundry stuff. She had a bag labeled dirty clothes hanging above her bed that was quite full and I unhooked it to bring it inside with me. The microwave beeped and I pulled out the popcorn. I grabbed one of Tux's doggy biscuits and slung the washing bag over my shoulder.

The wooden front door closed behind me from the force of the wind and Tux jumped up and came over to me. He was already wary of his surroundings and who was meant to be here.

"Here you go, buddy." I handed him the biscuit and he rubbed against my leg in thanks.

"Popcorn!" I dangled the bag in front of the girls and Cassie snatched it and tore the bag open.

They didn't say a word, the only sound they made was crunching and I knew they were happy.

"I'm just putting this in the laundry." I tried to whisper to Stella.

"No, I can do that." She jumped up from the mattress and met me in the hall.

"Don't be silly, you've been washing our clothes all afternoon. You can do your own here, saves you going to some creepy laundromat." I pressed.

"I like creepy laundromats." She joked.

"Well too bad." I began opening the bag and dumping it into a basket in the queue to be washed. Out of the corner of my eye, I spotted a black lacey thong on top of the pile and my nether region rejoiced.

"Dane!" She scolded as she mixed the clothes together, so her underwear wasn't showing.

"We all wear underwear, yours are just smaller than the rest of ours." I laughed.

She held her face in her hands as she wet bright red. "Okay, I'll do my washing here. When you're not around." She laughed.

The dryer beeped and Stella pulled out a basket full of my clothes and began folding them. "Leave them, I like them crinkly." I smiled.

"I may not iron, but I do fold." She sighed.

"What are you guys doing, you're missing the movie!" Cassie scolded us as she stood in the doorway.

"Sorry Cas, we're coming." Stella smiled at her and dropped what she was doing to follow her out.

I looked at the double mattress on the floor with the two squashed pillows that needed replacing and the new fluffy pink mink blanket Cassie had voluntarily offered us to share since we had been banished to the floor.

"Knew I should have got the girls bigger beds." I laughed as I took up most of the room and Stella was pinned between me and the corner of the couch where Tux was now lying as the girls all sprawled out to lay down.

"Lesson learned." She yawned.

Stella didn't bother to sit up, she lay on her side, her chest facing me. I could sense her eyes becoming heavy and I pulled an extra blanket off the side of the couch over her.

"Is she asleep?" Lilly whispered loudly in my ear.

"I think so." I nodded.

Tux was also snoring on the couch, once his mom was resting, he seemed to let his guard down a lot more and accepted an opportunity for sleep.

I got more comfortable on the mattress and laid down and pulled the extra blanket over myself after I removed my shirt.

"Stella, go to bed." I nudged her gently.

But she muttered nonsensical things I couldn't understand and after one more attempt, I decided to leave her. The movie dragged on, and the girls were all asleep on the couch also and I began picking each one up and carrying them to their beds, something I'd have to do quite often when I agreed to movie nights.

The last one was Stella. I bent down and picked her up and carried her to my bedroom. The blankets were already folded back, and the heated bed sheet stopped the sting of the cold from waking her. I turned the settings down and covered her up in the other blankets and she grabbed my arm.

"What are you doing?" She asked incoherently.

"I just put you in bed. Get some rest." I brushed the hair off her face.

She smiled sleepily and let my arm go. She looked so good in my bed. I wanted to climb in with her and do unspeakable things to her, but I walked myself back to the lounge room and now that the mattress was gone, I tried to sleep on the couch.

Stella

It was six am when I rolled over and checked my phone, I'd woken up before my alarm and I briefly remembered Dane picking me up and carrying me to the bed. It was a good thing I was so tired, or I might have asked him to stay. The house was quiet, but I fought the urge to stay in the warm soft bed so I could wash my face, brush my hair and teeth before the house began to busy with before-school chaos.

Once I was dressed, I roamed into the lounge room where Dane was sleeping with Tux half on his bare chest and arms wrapped around him.

I could hear a little giggle from Lilly as she spied on them from the hallway.

"Good morning mischief!" I whispered. "What do you say we get ready for the bus so Dad can have a little more sleep." I winked.

She nodded to agree. The older girls were already awake and dressed.

"What time do you guys leave?" I asked as I closed Audrey's door behind me.

"We go to before school care cause Dad has to start early some days, we get picked up at seven." Audrey explained.

"Okay, well you girls finish getting ready, I'll see what I can whip up for breakfast." I snuck out the door quietly.

In the fridge, there were six eggs left, some cheese, and a small pack of ham. The freezer had nothing more than the fresh diced onions from last night. I found a bowl, cracked all the eggs in with some cheese, diced the ham, and heated a pan to cook the omelets.

"What's that?" Cassie asked as she followed her nose into the kitchen.

"Ham and cheese omelet." I yawned.

Audrey and Lilly followed her, and they all sat at the bench quietly as I served them all a plate of omelet each and they devoured the lot.

"Thanks, Stella!" Audrey hugged me. "I think the bus is here. Come on." She whispered to Cassie and Lilly.

I opened and closed the door as quietly as I could so as not to wake Dane or Tux and I walked up the driveway with the girls, Lilly's hand in mine, and they each hugged me goodbye and thanked me for breakfast.

"See you at school." I waved as the bus drove off.

I went to my van and pulled out the last packet of bacon, four eggs, and a packet of pancake mix, the just-add-water kind. I headed back into the house, and I noticed Tux stirring.

"Shhh." I hushed him hoping he might settle a little longer.

"Too late." Dane's voice was a little hoarse.

"Sorry, I tried to let you sleep a little bit longer." I walked over and sat on the end of the couch.

"Fuck, what time is it?" He sat up rubbing his eyes.

"Just after seven, don't worry the girls were up and dressed when I was. I made them breakfast and walked them to the bus." I assured him.

"You did?" he smiled.

"Yes, take your time. Do you like pancakes, bacon, and eggs?" I said from the kitchen.

He followed me to the kitchen, and he sat on a stool at the kitchen island. I placed a black coffee in front of him and he wrapped his hands around it.

"I'll be a little more invisible this afternoon." I smiled.

"What do you mean?" he asked as I flipped the pancakes.

"We don't really know each other and somehow, I feel so at ease here, but I don't want to intrude on you and the girls. I need to do some shopping anyway so if it's cool, I'll go do that after school." I explained.

He looked up at me as he took another sip of the coffee and shook his head. " You seem to fit in well here, but don't feel like you need to ask permission to do anything, we're the adults in this house. You are free to come and go as you please, as long as the girls are happy, my home is open to you." He smiled.

"Thank you, but I will sleep in my van tonight, as comfy as your bed is." I laughed.

"It's big enough for two." He grinned playfully.

Ughh, he was so handsome with his bed hair, shirtless, and his flannel pants covered in my dog's fur. The only thing stopping me from throwing my body at him was a hot pan and a plate of crispy bacon, I was hungrier for the bacon.

I glared at him from across the bench as I picked at the bacon, he didn't let my eyes go. "It wouldn't be a good idea for us to share a bed." I mumbled.

"Of course not, the girls might get the wrong idea…" He agreed, but he still held my gaze.

"We should probably get ready for work." I suggested as I stuffed a pancake in my mouth.

The sexual tension kept building and Dane stood up and leaned over me to place his mug in the sink.

"I guess we should." He was so close to me now that I could feel the warmth from his chest and hear his breathing become heavier.

"Did you bring some clothes inside?" he whispered into my ear.

I nodded as his arms closed around me still holding the bench on either side of the sink. "Dane…" I breathed softly. I had nothing to say, and my mouth wasn't occupied with food anymore.

He raised his hand and brushed my cheek and I melted into his touch.

"We're going to be late." I whispered.

He picked me up and I wrapped my legs around him as he kissed my neck and cupped my ass with his hands and carried me into his room.

He placed me down on the bed and kissed me softly on the lips. "I want to do this, but we'll be so late if we do, raincheck?" He smiled.

"We can meet in the van tonight." I winked. " Once the kids are asleep, Tux will guard them." I smiled.

"Nine on the dot, wear that lacey thong. I can't stop imagining you in it." He laughed as he pulled his pants over his boner.

I grabbed my clothes and raced to the bathroom to change and brush my hair out.

Not even two minutes later he was behind me as I was slipping a shirt over my head. He appeared behind me in the mirror dressed in taupe pants, a navy shirt, and a cream woolen sweater over the top of that, he straightened his collar in the mirror as I brushed through my hair.

"You aren't deterring any single mums in that outfit." I teased.

He smiled at me in the mirror as he dampened his hair into something befitting what he wore.

"I'm not interested in them." He tousled some of my waves.

"One time only, let's just get it out of our systems. Then back to business." I sucked in a deep breath as I turned to face him.

"Oh, businesswoman." He smiled. "I respect that, I'm in the middle of a nasty divorce, you deserve better than a divorcee with three kids." He became more serious.

"Not an age thing, just a *I can't be tied down thing'* given how I live my life." I softened my words as I used my hands expressively.

"No, I get it. One night. That's all we get." He agreed.

I offered my hand in a handshake position, and he took it and shook it and we continued to get ready and left together.

We arrived at school and went our separate ways down the hall and into each of our classrooms. There was already a hoard of concerned mothers lurking outside Dane's door. With a name like Dane De La Roche and his perfectly chiseled jaw, he was a hot topic around the school, some of the teachers would even talk about him in the lunchroom.

I had a kindergarten class today and I dreaded my whole afternoon ahead. I needed to do some shopping but if I was having this crazy sex appointment tonight, I needed to get all the dormant parts of my body freshened up.

The bell rang as the day ended and I began to walk home skipping out on the ride with Dane and the girls and hoping I'd get home to get my van before they got back.

It was almost a sprint, but I got back puffed out, but in time to unhook my van, put away the cables and hose, and wave to Tux through the windows and promise him treats. I set off into town and found a small salon to get my legs and Brazilian waxed.

"Hi, can I get the whole Brazilian and full leg wax please?" I said to the lady at reception.

"Come through." She nodded.

She walked me into a white room and asked me to remove my pants and underwear and freshen up with the wet wipes provided and then use a warm flannel to remove any residue.

Another lady came in and greeted me and confirmed the services I'd asked for. She worked on my legs first, that was the easy part. It wasn't long till she moved to the Brazilian and I braced like I was about to be struck by a truck.

"Relax…" she patted my arm.

"I'll try." I squeaked. She giggled a little but didn't drag out the process and applied the first layers of wax. I may have passed out after that. It was a blur, but I came out with a Sphynx kitty instead of the Persian I had gone in with and I paid and tipped both the ladies.

"Thank you!" I waved goodbye after making a return appointment.

There was a Cub grocer not too far away and I made my way over and grabbed a cart and began filling it with some fruit and vegetables, a few different cuts of meat, various other things, and a bottle of red wine.

When I was done, I headed straight back to the house, parked the van, and began hooking up the hose and cables again.

"Get her!" Lilly yelled as Tux raced outside and tackled me in the freshly mowed grass and I held him close. But this made him crazy every time and soon he was doing zoomies over the lawn, I sat up to watch him with Lilly as she plucked grass and leaves out of my hair.

"Thanks, Lil, how was your day today?" I asked.

"It was good, I made some new friends, and they invited me to sit with them in the cafeteria, I had the sausage pizza." She smiled as she reflected on her day.

"I'm really glad to hear that." I swung my arm around her and hugged her.

"How was your day?" She smiled at me.

"I was in the kindergarten room today; those little kids are all very cute. It's hard to be cross when they do the wrong thing." I laughed.

"Ugh, little kids are so annoying." She grunted and I chuckled aloud at her disgusted but empathic notion of me. "I wish you were in my class; our helper is Mr. Daniels. He smells like too much aftershave." She added.

"If we're lucky they might do a rotation." I said.

"It's not fair! Dad gets you in his class and Audrey too!" she huffed.

"But I get to see you at home too. Maybe you wouldn't like me as a teacher's assistant?" I quizzed her.

"You do have a point, here I get you almost all to myself." She hugged me tightly.

Dane stood in the doorway still in his work clothes as he watched Tux run zoomies and Lilly and I cuddle in the grass.

"I ordered pizzas." Dane shouted across the grass. I approved with a thumbs up and threw Lilly over my shoulder and walked her inside as she thrashed and giggled.

"Stella!" She begged. "Daddy help!" she laughed some more.

I placed her down on her feet and she tickled me back and quickly ran off to the bathroom. Dane smiled at me with his bright eyes and pulled another blade of grass out of my hair.

"Bit of a hot mess there Stella." He winked.

"You have no idea…" I teased as I brushed past him and beelined for the laundry to resume my duties.

Dane went to his room and undressed into nothing but a towel and came into the laundry to drop off his work clothes from the day.

My jaw dropped when he flashed me his perfect chest and I felt a weakness in my knees as my eyes trailed to his forbidden place.

"That's not fair!" I threw a peg at him.

"One night only baby." He stroked his cock as I moved closer desperate to feel him.

"One whole night…" I pulled his hand away and teased the tip of him with my fingers.

He closed his towel and pulled it back over just in time as Lilly sprung into the laundry room with a handful of clothes, she was wrapped in a towel twice her size, her hair dripping water over the floor.

"Fuck." Dane screeched as he turned his back to Lilly and raced off to the shower.

"What's his problem?" Audrey appeared.

"He needs to put two dollars in the jar!" Cassie clapped as she followed Audrey.

"I think he had a rough day. He might just need a good soak in the bath." I explained through my teeth.

"Well, he could have at least waited till the rest of us had showered." Audrey growled.

There was a loud knock at the door and Tux howled and hammered his way to the front of the house and I ran after him with the girls.

"The money is on the table." Dane shouted through the bathroom door.

I grabbed the cash and paid the teenager who delivered the four large pizzas.

"Thank you." I smiled as he handed me the change and I closed the door and set down the hot pizzas on the bench.

"Lilly, go change we'll wait for you." I ordered as she shivered in her wet towel.

"Okay." She agreed.

"Wait for me too!" Dane shouted from the bathroom.

Audrey began tapping her fingers on the bench while she waited. The smell escaped the closed pizza boxes as I guarded them.

Dane came out first in shorts and a shirt and Lilly in a nightie. "Dig in." Dane approved as I opened the first box.

The girls sat on the couch as they ate their cheese and pepperoni pizzas and Dane snuck Tux pieces of sausage and pepperoni.

"If he vomits, you're cleaning it up." I grinned.

"He'll be fine, look at the size of him!" he protested.

I nodded to agree and shrugged my shoulders.

Tux was four years old and one hundred and thirty pounds, he was one of the biggest in his litter and he'd been well-trained in water sports and had excellent survival and rescue skills. A dog was my must-have when I decided to travel alone, not only for companionship but because my goal was to kayak every possible body of water I could find in my two-seater kayak. That stayed strapped to the van's roof secured on the roof racks that had a pully system to help me get it back onto the roof when I was done.

So far, I'd traveled from Washington state across the top of the USA. I'd planned the trip with my best friend as a kid, but she didn't see life past the age of nineteen. She was hit by a drunk driver while walking home from work one night. The crime scene was so gruesome she was only identifiable by her dental records. The driver died too, he was thrown through the windshield as he struck a pole on the back end, the car kept spinning out and that's when it hit Ana. I sobbed for months and months until my dad found my old Sprinter van second-hand for sale a few streets over. He encouraged me to defer college indefinitely and to live a life memorable for both of us.

So, in that sense, Tux filled Ana's place. It was the same kayak we carried together every summer down to Matthew's Beach Park. We grew up three streets away from each other and saw each other almost every day. To say we were inseparable would be an understatement, she was a limb I didn't know I needed until I lost her.

Three months into the grief it was almost fall and I realized being home was what made her loss ache so much more. I dipped into my college fund and planned out how to remodel the van, I knew I would find myself in places I didn't want to leave my van. I wanted it to be discreet, comfortable, and have enough resources to get me through at least a week on a rough turn. I had buttonhole surveillance cameras installed that were barely noticeable, solar panels, roof racks, a tiny sink, a bathroom, a composting toilet, a comfortable bed, and loads of storage.

Then my mom surprised me with Tux at that three-month mark. He was supposed to be their dog, and I remember how excited she had been to get him. He was going to be their new child once I went to college. They'd always wanted a Newfoundland, but I remember the way my mom said *'you need him more'* when she placed him in my arms, her eyes muddled with tears.

He came with enrollments in swimming classes and training for a variety of other things. She had waited a lifetime and a three-year waitlist for Tux and without a second thought she gave him to me. Her heart was big like that. When she loved, she loved hard. She gave unconditionally, with no expectations. My father was a military man, he was hard to the bone with a soft exterior. This dog was their celebration of children grown and raised well. But now he was mine, he was my new best friend.

As long as the classes took, it also took me to complete the van and it was a surprisingly great way for Tux and me to bond. He followed me as I wrestled with the kayak one morning down to the water, I was determined to do this alone even though my dad was itching to help me from the shoreline holding an empty leash. But it was the first time without Ana and the weight was unbalanced. Tux stepped into the water and pulled himself up into the kayak as my dad watched on and the kayak balanced out and he sat upright, so gracefully in the front seat. I think that was the moment I knew we were ready to go. Tux had a way of knowing what I needed, and he was fiercely protective but in the same breath so gentle and caring. I had everything I could need except a life vest for Tux.

Shopping for a life vest of Tux's size and expected growth proved to be challenging and took several attempts but we finally found one and that set the date. I had dinner two days later with my family and Ana's came along also to see me off. I left the next morning. I've been gone for almost four years now. I don't think I'll ever find my way back to Washington. I'd found a nomadic way of living, working only when I needed to, if I needed to. Sometimes I'd like a place enough to stay for six or so months, but I always moved on. I took jobs with short shifts, waitressing, and lifeguard in summer at local pools. They'd often let me park my van in their car parks and stay until it was time for me to move on. Tux got plenty of love from kitchen staff and often ended up with more food than he could eat, even for a dog of his gargantuan size.

I looked up from my food and I'd devoured four slices and Tux was staring at me as he licked the pepperoni juices off his lips. I was perched on a bar stool at the bench and the sound of giggling girls filled my ears as Dane cracked jokes and made silly faces with his pizza.

"Bedtime soon, buddy." I patted Tux as I offered him a doggy biscuit.

"NO! Can't you stay?" Cassie shouted as she heard me talking to Tux.

"I live right out front." I laughed as I moved closer to them.

"Will you be making breakfast tomorrow?" Lilly asked.

"Lilly!" Dane hushed her.

"I'd love to make you breakfast, but when can I get in on these cereal videos?" I winked at Dane.

"Saturday we are allowed to film, this week we are doing one called 'Milo' it's from Australia!" Audrey cooed.

"All the way from Australia?" I smiled.

"Yes, we have fans from down under." Lilly flicked her hair back.

"Don't worry. PO Box." Dane assured me.

"They sent Tim Tam's too; Daddy ate them all." Cassie scowled at him.

"Well, maybe we can order some online and you can show me what all the hype is about with those cookies." I pulled her hair back and loosely braided it.

"We could include them in our video!" Lilly lined up behind Cassie and held up a hair tie for me.

"I'd like two braids, please. I'd like to have curly hair for school tomorrow." She ordered.

"What do you say?" Dane whispered.

"Please Stella?" she smiled sweetly.

"Of course, I can." I agreed.

I secretly loved having all this hair to play with. Ana and I spent hours as kids styling each other's hair and watching Adam Sandler movies.

I finished with Lilly's hair and Audrey was next, she had two long socks and a YouTube tutorial open on her iPad with how to wrap her hair so it would be soft bouncy waves in the morning.

"Audrey, that seems complicated." Dane rubbed his forehead a little embarrassed.

"Do you think I can't do it?" I joked.

Dane put his hands up to defend himself as he backed away slowly with the empty plates.

"You're such a sassy pants daddy!" Lilly teased.

"Woah, I'll just leave you ladies alone then." He retreated to the kitchen to clean up.

I watched the video, wrapped Audrey's hair in the socks, and secured them so she could sleep comfortably. They all stood before me, posed with their hair, and hugged me to thank me before rushing off to their bedrooms. They all had their rooms, but Dane had put them into Cassie's room so we could paint the other rooms this weekend.

"Goodnight Stella." Lilly squeezed me.

"Goodnight beautiful girls." I pulled the other two in for a hug, and I watched as they went to hug Dane and Tux.

The girls bounded off to their room and snapped the door shut and I heard more giggles and protesting about who would sleep where.

"Still up for it?" Dane moved closer to me but far enough away to be cautious not to crowd my personal space.

"I am, if you are." I closed the space between us and touched his chest. Even through a shirt, I could see his definition.

"See you in half an hour?" he brushed my cheek.

"See you there." I winked as I turned for the front door and Tux followed.

Dane

Half an hour later the girls were finally asleep and Stella's light in the van was still on. I exited the front door softly as Tux wandered inside and made himself at home on the couch.

I wandered over the lawn and knocked softly on Stella's door, and she slid it open seconds later. She seemed nervous but welcomed me inside and I kissed her forehead softly. I felt her close her eyes and she fell into my chest.

"One night, that's all I have in me." she whispered as my hands found hers.

"We don't have to do this if you don't want to…" I sighed as I felt a slight resistance from her.

"No, I want to. I think I need to, but we need to be clear about where we stand." She assured me.

"Hi, I'm Dane. I'm signing divorce papers next week." I smiled as I pulled her chin up to me.

"I'm Stella, an emotionally and geographically unavailable gypsy." She laughed.

"Nice to meet you." I pressed my lips to hers and she draped her arms around my neck.

I pulled her thighs into my hands and soon she was sitting on the benchtop, her hands were pulling my shirt off and she gasped as she clawed softly at my chest.

"You're not just a teacher…" she sucked in a breath.

"I was a SEAL before this." I laughed as I pulled her hair to one side and sucked softly on her neck.

"That explains it." She hissed as I tickled her accidentally.

"Do you have a condom?" she asked.

"FUCK!" I growled.

She brushed her hands through my hair and held me in her eyes as she traced her hands down to rub at the bulge in my shorts that was quickly dying off after I realized he wouldn't be coming out to play tonight. I pulled her hands away and wrapped my hands around her back and caressed her soft skin.

"Sorry, I didn't think of that." I grumbled. "Do you have anything?" I added.

"I don't normally do this…" she sighed.

"Oh?" I was curious.

"I just don't ever make time for guys." She blushed unintentionally as she hopped down off the bench.

"Raincheck?" she snapped before I could say anything.

"Sure." I smiled.

She lay on the bed behind us and patted the empty spot beside her for me and I climbed up and I lay beside her in the crisp cold van. She pulled a fleece blanket over us and lay facing me. I threw an arm over her, and she slipped a leg between mine.

"Well, since we can't fuck, wanna tell me a little about you?" I smiled.

"You're probably a lot more interesting than I am." She laughed.

"Rock, paper, scissors." She made a fist and held it out to meet mine.

Three rounds later I had defeated her shamelessly and I took a deep breath and pondered how to give her the whole story in a light version.

"Where do I start…" I sighed.

"You don't have to tell me anything you're uncomfortable with." She traced the lines on the back of my hand. It felt so organic with her and as close as she was right now, she was completely out of my grasp.

"My wife cheated, got knocked up, and left us. We moved out here for a fresh start." I said softly.

She gasped and sighed all in one breath. "I'm sorry." She moved her hand up my arm, pulled her body closer to me, and rubbed my shoulder.

"I'm glad it happened, Stella. I had known for years, I just allowed it because I felt like I was wrong for leaving her and the girls every time I went to work. She found comfort elsewhere and I got to blow things up as an outlet. Real healthy huh?" I grinned.

"I can't pretend to know what any of that's like, but I can tell you from an outsider's perspective, you're doing good." She smiled.

"I hope so, they deserve so much more than what they got from her. I haven't exactly been around most of their lives either." I sighed.

"You're enough, I can see it." She said encouragingly.

"Maybe, Audrey's like a live-in bodyguard." I laughed.

"She'll fight off all the bad ones." She laughed.

"What's next for you when you leave here?" I asked.

"Whatever really, there's no real plan. Just wake up in a new place each day." She smiled.

"Good to do it while you're young." I nodded.

"Yeah, it was always the plan." She smiled falsely. Her eyes pooled a little and I sensed pain in the tone of her voice as it cracked a little.

"Who was the guy?" I brushed her nose with my thumb.

"No guy." She laughed.

"Phew…" I joked. Or was it?

"My turn?" she questioned.

"Spill it…" I pressed.

"My best friend died, but it was always our plan to do this together. So, I had to do it, you know? for both of us." Her eyes became heavier, and her voice began to catch a little, and I noticed a photo on the wall behind her of two teenage girls in graduation caps.

"Can I ask how?" I said bravely.

"Drunk driver." She replied.

Her face was wet with tears now. She huddled the blanket into her face as she tried to hide her despair. I pulled her into my chest and held her as she wept silently.

I got it, no more words were necessary. How could you ever feel normal after that? At her age your best friend was a part of your body, you weren't meant to part like that. You were meant to find the love of your life in another pair of best friends, marry in the same year, and have babies that would be clones of their mothers or fathers.

"I'm sorry you had to go through that." I rubbed her back.

"It was years ago; I don't know why I still do this." She sat up disappointed in herself for crying.

"Because you only get one, maybe two of those friendships if you're lucky." I sat up beside her. "You'll never stop grieving, but you'll get better at it." I added.

"You're such a dad." She laughed.

"No, don't think of me like that. Not until I've had my way with you." I laughed.

"Dane I'm sorry if I've been too much. I kinda just blew in here out of nowhere and invaded your life, home, and work." She sighed.

"I think we work well together. In life, home, and work." I smiled.

"Thank you for saying that." She wiped her face with her hands.

"You've been a big help. I've never done this stuff alone. I don't know how to braid hair or cook meals they like.

You were a bonus and the girls like this place because you're here. I didn't think they'd let you in. Goes to show how well I know my daughter's." I sighed.

"It's new, you get to learn about each other all over again. That's special, you get to mold them from here." She smiled.

Stella had a way about her. She made me feel good about myself even when I was doing a terrible job. She was picking up the slack in my life like I never could. I was never able to get the grease stains out of Lilly's clothes and like witchcraft Stella had it sorted before I could even bring it up as an issue.

For the first time since we'd moved to Duluth the laundry pile was at an acceptable height. Food was being cooked in our kitchen and she had even been the excuse to mow the lawns.

A knock banged against the van door. "Stella!" Shouted Audrey and she shone a flashlight through the window as Tux scratched against the step beside her.

Stella jumped up and opened the door. "Everything okay?" She sunk to her level with concern.

"Yeah, Lilly wet the bed. Cassie got soaked." She giggled.

"Oh dear." I sighed.

"I'll come help." Stella shut off her lights and locked up the van and met us in the mudroom entry to the house.

"You wanna get her showered? I'll strip the bedding." She beelined for the linen cupboard which she'd soon find to be empty.

"Okay, empty. Let's work on that tomorrow." She took a mental note out loud.

We walked into the room the girls had been sharing and Lilly was sitting on the end of the bed with her robe around her as she cried.

"I'm sorry." She wailed.

"Lil, it's okay. Accidents happen all the time. You just need a shower, and we'll fix this up while you're in there." I kissed her on the nose.

"Really?" She looked up at me.

"You're in a new place Lil, it's okay to have accidents. Your body is probably still a little anxious." Stella said, she sat beside her and wrapped an arm around Lilly's shoulder.

"You don't have to wash it. He can." She pointed at me.

Stella laughed. "You know I don't mind at all, Tux used to wet the bed all the time when he was little. I'm a pro!" She assured her.

"Come on, shower time." I pulled her up and walked with her to the bathroom as Stella stripped the bedding with Cassie who was in a towel from a quick shower herself, Audrey was also helping her peel the wet sheets off.

"Okay, you can use that one. That's the good stuff." I winked as I pointed to the strawberry shower gel we only used for special occasions.

Cassie raced through the hallway with the pile of dirty sheets and Stella hunted through the linen box in my room.

"Dane?" She called.

I approached the room to see her on the floor battling through a pile of scrunched-up fitted sheets as she tried to find one the right size.

"Yeah?" I giggled as she huffed.

"Any idea which one might fit?" she sighed.

"Argh, I think one of those clear containers has some flat sheets. Let's just do that for the night." I scratched my head as I tried to recall the contents of the boxes and containers.

Stella pulled out a king-size flat sheet and took it to the room the girls were sharing. I followed behind her and we examined the true damage.

"I think we better move you girls into the lounge for the night. That's well and truly soaked through." I sighed.

Stella nodded as she began to haul it out of the room, not wasting any time. I grabbed the front end pulled it and Cassie grabbed the middle while Audrey opened the backdoor.

"Does this mean we get new beds?" Cassie clasped her hands together as if she were praying.

Audrey's ears pricked up and Stella held her hand over her mouth as she tried not to laugh.

"I guess you girls do deserve an upgrade of some sort. Is a new bed each what you'd like?" I was confused that the girls would want new beds and not a PS5 each.

"Can we still paint our rooms?" Audrey asked.

"I guess so." I agreed reluctantly.

"Go and write down your requests, I'll go get the paint tomorrow." Stella smiled.

"You sure that's how you want to spend your day off?" I turned to her and asked.

"I like home renovations. Told you I was handy, didn't I?" She turned to walk inside.

The girls were standing over a notepad on the counter each noting down their dream rooms.

"You have no idea what you just signed up for." I laughed at Stella.

"Signed up for what?" Lilly appeared.

"Thanks, Lil!" Cassie swooped her into a hug.

"What did I do?" Lilly asked, all confused.

"Dad said we can get new beds!" Audrey beamed.

"And remind me how that turned into whole new rooms, with paint?" I pondered aloud.

"We deserve upgrades…Your words." Cassie grinned as she wavered her piece of paper over my face.

"She got you there." Stella laughed.

"OK, pick your colors or themes and go to sleep in my bed. I'll take the lounge." I yawned.

"I'm going to retreat to my van." Stella squeezed my arm.

"Goodnight, sorry." I squeezed her hand back. She gave me a forgiving smile and headed for the front door with Tux in tow.

Stella

I heard the girls wandering past my van as I wrapped myself a little tighter in my blanket while the bus pulled up to collect them. I tossed and turned twice more and allowed myself a few more hours of sleep and when I woke it was past nine am.

Dane would be at school by now and when I opened the door there was an envelope with a key tucked inside it sitting on my step.

The air was brisk but not too windy and I pulled on some clothes and headed into the house, brushed my teeth, hair and washed my face then collected the girls' notes for the counter.

Lilly wanted a lilac room with gold trims like a princess. Cassie wanted a curtained bed with teal walls, woodsy, fairy-themed, and silver written in capitals and underlined. Audrey showed me how grown up she was with her description. Study desk, lots of books, greys, and pastel pinks.

Easy, I'd grab a few things from the thrift store and cheap paint from Walmart and mix my own colors with their basic range.

Dane had left his credit card with a note that said, *'Thank you'* and the card's PIN beneath it.

I'm heading over to Walmart. Do you need anything?

No, but do you want to take the truck? Call into class if you want the keys.

That might be wise. Walking over now.

I gathered the lists for reference and tucked them into my satchel and let Tux into the backyard before I locked up and began walking to the school.

When I arrived, I peeked into the classroom through the window, so I didn't disrupt the students. Dane spotted me and pulled the keys from his bottom drawer and cracked the door open enough to hand me the keys.

"We'll walk home if you're going to be busy." He smiled.

"I can pick you up." I nodded.

"No, I think the girls would like it. They've been asking about stopping at the park just up the road.

"Call me if you change your mind." I agreed.

"Thank you, Stella." Dane went to reach for me but pulled himself back.

"Don't thank me yet." I curled my bottom lip with worry.

"You'll do great, don't rush. I'll help when I get home." He turned back to the class and sighed as the kids began to muck around.

"That's my cue. See you tonight." I waved goodbye.

I started the truck and punched in the address for Walmart and set off into the heart of the town.

Once there I grabbed a cart and scanned the store for items, I could use to decorate the girls' rooms before I found the paint section. Wallpaper popped out in front of me, and I browsed through to find anything that could fit their themes.

A purple and gold damask pattern for Lilly for her princess room. A magical lake with fairy lights which was far too big for Cassie, I'd have to trim it to size. Finally, a light floral pattern that would match Audrey's wishes and meet all the colors she wanted.

I headed to the paint section and ordered the paint I'd need and some empty buckets, brushes, and rollers.

On my way to the till there was a bountiful section of fake greenery, and I fished through for flowers, vines, and ostrich feathers.

Once I had a good selection of décor, I finished walking to the till paid for all the items in my cart and loaded them into the truck, and made my way back to Dane's house.

Dane must have emptied the rooms of furniture this morning, it was all stacked neatly on the outdoor patio. I laid down some old newspaper sheets on the floors of the rooms so I could mix my colors and start outlining the walls that would be painted. The bedrooms were all white, so I didn't apply a base layer.

Audrey's room was first. I mixed a pale pink peach and began slathering three walls with it on the roller. Next was Lilly, her color came out as a beautiful lilac.

An hour passed and her walls were done. I was thrilled when I stood back to watch it dry in the breeze from the open window. It would need a second coat soon. While the first coat dried, I mixed the color for Cassie's room. The teal color popped magnificently over the hardwood floors.

Soon I could hear the girls giggling from the open window as I finished painting the final wall in Cassie's room. I lay on the floor covered in paint as the breeze wafted through the open window and chilled the beads of sweat on my forehead as I caught my breath from scaling my way down the ladder.

"Oh! It stinks in here!" I heard Lilly shout.

"You're not allowed in any of the rooms!" Dane reminded them.

I quickly cater pillared over the floor and shut the door with my foot.

"Stella?" Dane knocked on the door.

"All clear?" I asked before he opened the door.

"Yep!" He turned the handle and entered the room.

"Woah! You did well." He looked around the room marveling. "This is a great color; she's going to love it." He complimented me.

"Ugh, I hope so. I can't feel my shoulders." I said as I struggled to pull myself up and stretched my arms out.

"I'll stop by and give you a massage tonight." He reached a hand to me and pulled me up.

"Don't touch me, I'm covered in paint." I held my hand over his chest as he almost leaned in to kiss me.

"Good point." He leaned back as he looked around the room. "What's with the one white wall?" He asked.

I yawned as I pointed at the rolls of wallpaper in the middle of the room.

"Going to need your help with that part." I smiled.

He pulled off his jacket and leaned down to peel a roll open.

"Not now, we need to wait till this is all dry." I rested my hand on the roll to stop him.

"Dinner?" His thumb stroked my cheek as I watched his lips move.

"I'm starving." I confessed.

"Italian?" Dane asked.

"As long as that's what the girls want." I smiled against the warmth of his hand on my face.

Dane walked out of the room and called for the girls as I followed behind him and Lilly's jaw dropped as she caught sight of me with spots of paint all over my clothes.

"Oh, my goodness…It's happening!" She squealed with excitement.

"Give us a few more days to get it all done. Stella can't do it all in one day." Dane reminded Lilly.

"One room I could. Probably not three though." I laughed. "What do you say to it Italian for dinner?" I smiled.

"Alfredo?" Audrey's ears pricked up.

"And lasagna?" Cassie gleamed.

"Lilly?" Dane pressed for suggestions from her.

"Hmmm, how about some garlic bread?" She nodded.

"Sounds delicious!" Dane lifted her to hug her.

"Okay, girls go shower while I ring the restaurant. You too!" He looked at me in my dirty clothes as he scrunched his face animatedly at me.

"Yes, boss." I scoffed as I walked myself to the laundry to get the girls all some clean towels.

I heard Dane on the phone as I walked out the door and to my van to shower. I turned on the shower and sat on my compostable toilet while the hot water soothed my aching shoulders while I washed the paint off my face and hands.

"Stella, you okay to watch the girls while I go get the food?" he said after he knocked.

"Yeah, give me five." I flicked my hair into a towel and pulled on an oversized shirt that was more like a dress after roughly drying myself and my favorite pair of 'granny undies'.

I slipped on some Ugg boots and strolled back to the house where Cassie and Lilly were arguing over who would shower next. Audrey was propped on the end of the couch combing out her wet her and I went to join her.

"I won't be long." Dane messed Audrey's hair teasingly.

"DAD! Don't mess with the hair." She glared at him unimpressed, and I chuckled a little to myself, he smirked at me as he walked around to me, but I defended myself with my own hairbrush.

"Party poopers!" He poked out his tongue and turned to collect his keys and headed out the front door.

Audrey jumped up and turned on the TV, connected to Spotify, and turned on some music. Taylor Swift's 'Long Live' played and she swayed her body as she finished brushing her hair.

"I love this song!" Cassie screamed as she bounced into the lounge room shouting the lyrics.

"I didn't realize this was a *Swiftie* household!" I smiled wide.

"Dad hates it." Cassie laughed.

Audrey paused. "Do you like her too?" Her eyes homed in on me quite seriously and I felt like I was being interrogated.

"Ummmm." I let them hang on to my words a moment too long and Lilly appeared in a towel. I cleared my throat and began to sing lyrics from Willow. The girls hung onto every word, and they grabbed my hands as we skipped around the room.

"Okay, Cassie go shower. Lilly, go and get dressed. We should be able to squeeze in another song before dinner.

"One that goes for ten minutes and thirteen seconds?" Audrey questioned.

"Only if you can sing it without the lyrics." I snickered.

"Oh Stella, you're new. We'll forgive you." Lilly started brushing her hair as she walked to the laundry to find some clean pajamas.

"Are you serious?" My eyes widened at the thought of how many times I had personally tried to nail that song and failed miserably every time I lost ten minutes of my life down a highway to the breakup anthem of the century.

Cassie seemed to rush her shower and she didn't spare a second. She raced to the laundry and threw on whatever was in the clean basket I hadn't yet folded.

"Audrey! HIT IT!" Cassie ordered as she leaped onto the couch and grabbed my hairbrush to use as a microphone while Audrey typed in the title. Lilly was rummaging through the kitchen drawer and came back with two wooden spoons. One for her, one for me. Audrey stood on the couch with her hairbrush, and she began to sing sweetly and softly as the music built and soon the room was filled with the girls dancing and singing into their makeshift microphones.

The girls were singing to All Too Well when a ball of paper smacked me in the face as I came out of the moment of screaming lyrics with the girls and dancing around the room with Lilly on my back.

Audrey paused the music and froze a little embarrassed at the presence of Dane in the room.

Daddy…" Lilly grinned as she dumped her wooden spoon in his arms.

"Good show, girls!" I clapped as I breezed past Dane towards the kitchen.

"That was so much FUN!" Cassie was tugging at Audrey who was still bright red.

"You? A Swiftie?" Dane leaned over the bench and held my gaze.

"She raised my generation. She is mother!" I laughed.

"MOTHER!" Cassie swooned at me speaking her language and she comically bowed, and Lilly copied her.

Dane laughed as he turned his focus to Audrey.

"I didn't know you could sing like that. Why don't you sing for me?" Dane asked softly but with such pride in his voice. He wasn't wrong, she was an incredible singer.

"I'm shy." She snorted.

"But you sang for Stella?" He questioned.

"I didn't mean to, it just happened." She shrugged her shoulders.

I grabbed some plates and cutlery and began plating everyone's food up and taking the plates to the dining table.

"The food smells amazing!" I said as the girls followed me to the table and started eating.

Lilly swirled spaghetti around her fork and placed it on top of her slice of garlic bread. Cassie and Audrey were shoveling Alfredo down so fast it could have been a competition and I got to work on a slice of extra-large lasagna.

Dane's eyes lovingly traced the room with pride as he seemed to absorb the peace and serenity of happy children and full bellies.

"Movie?" Cassie asked.

"Tomorrow. You girls could use an early night." Dane yawned.

"Stella, will you watch a movie with us tomorrow?" Lilly asked.

"Only if it's a Halloween movie." I bounced my eyebrows cheekily.

"Hocus Pocus!" Cassie exclaimed.

"Dad, we need to work on our costumes for the Halloween Dance." Lilly reminded him.

"Dance?" I asked.

"Ugh, yeah. We were told today. The PTA is holding a themed Halloween ball." He cringed at the idea.

"What's the theme?" I asked.

"They said nothing too spooky. It's woodsy fairytale." Dane groaned.

"I'm going to be a green fairy like Tinkerbell." Lilly said.

"What about you two?" I turned to Audrey and Cassie.

"I'll do pink." Cassie wasn't bothered and shrugged her shoulders at the idea.

"I'll do blue." Audrey said with a little more maturity in her voice.

"What about you?" I nudged Dane under the table with my foot.

"Any suggestions?" He nudged me back.

"How about a centaur?" I chuckled.

"Got half a horse lying around somewhere?" He laughed.

"We could incorporate Tux into it." I joked.

"Funny! Next?" Dane laughed.

"Okay, what about a faun...you wouldn't even need a shirt." I smiled.

"Dad, you should definitely wear a shirt." Cassie growled.

"The mothers had good intentions with this theme." I teased.

"What are you wearing, Stella?" Dane said loudly to put me on the spot.

"Oh, I'm not going." I laughed.

"Yes, you are. I need a date, slash bodyguard." Dane huffed.

"We'll be your bodyguards daddy." Cassie smiled.

"But don't you think Stella should come? She's a staff member too." He said with sarcasm as he tried to persuade the girls to force me to go.

"He has a point, Stella." Audrey laughed.

"Fine. I'll go as a nymph!" I kicked Dane under the table playfully.

He choked on his food and spat it into a napkin.

"What's a nymph?" Cassie asked as she slapped Dane on the back.

"Ask your dad." I grinned.

His eyes bulged with tears as he drank some water and shook his head at me.

"Nymphs are just adult-sized fairies." He said shortly.

I locked my eyes on my plate as I stroked his leg with my foot underneath the table.

"Some nymphs are naughty." He laughed.

"Same with Fauns, they can't all be trusted." I added to his comment.

"So, it's settled! You'll be a Faun." Lilly stood up from the table with her empty plate.

"What do nymphs wear?" Cassie was curious.

"Mostly green, very earthy tones." I smiled.

"Can we go shopping for costumes online?" Audrey grinned at Dane.

"Why online?" Dane questioned.

"They definitely won't have any standout costumes here." Her expression was serious as she glowered at him to agree.

"Okay, grab my laptop." He sighed.

The girls huddled together as they scanned the internet for costumes. None of them saw anything they liked and soon they were filled with disappointment.

"Why don't you guys just buy some plain dresses and then we can go to Michael's and get some cool stuff to jazz them up?" I suggested.

"You can sew?" Lilly squealed.

"No, not exactly. I can glue some jewels on and stuff." I took a deep breath as I defended myself.

"Now you've done it…" Dane whispered.

"She'll learn." Audrey squeezed Lilly's shoulders. "That or dad can do it." She grinned cheekily.

"Okay, I think it's bedtime." Dane was tense at the thought of such a massive undertaking.

I packed the leftover food away into disposable containers Dane had purchased from Walmart and stashed everything into the fridge and began washing dishes while Dane kissed the girl's goodnight as he tucked them into his bed.

It was a rather early night for them, but Dane seemed exhausted. Maybe he'd had a rougher than usual day or maybe this single parenting gig was just getting on top of him.

Dane went to shower as I was finishing up the dishes and I went to inspect the girls' bedrooms and see how much of the paint was dry and which walls may need a second coat of paint.

Lilly's room was fine. Even with the large workers spotlight beaming in the room it was a beautiful shade of purple. I pulled the ladder in from Audrey's room, unrolled the peel-and-stick sheet of wallpaper, and one by one began sticking them onto the feature wall.

Ten or so minutes passed, and I'd laid several sheets when Dane sprung into the room with a singlet that showed off all his muscles and underwear that left nothing to the imagination.

 "Nope, get out! I can't do distractions right now. If you want to help, you need more clothes than that." I squinted my eyes together playfully.

Dane approached the ladder and I turned to face him, and he gripped my hips. I wrapped my arms around his neck, and he pulled me down from the ladder and placed me gently on the ground.

"I'm not here to ravish you, Stella. I'm here to take over the peel and sticking, you've done a lot already." He pecked my forehead and then brushed past me softly as he climbed the ladder with a roll of wallpaper in his hand.

"I can handle this!" I scoffed.

"I know you can, but you aren't doing it alone." He smiled back at me.

But alone was what I was used to. Four years now and I have done everything alone. I'd changed tires alone, filled my oil, changed my wiper blades. I'd eat alone in restaurants, and go to the cinema alone. I couldn't bring

Tux to do a lot of things so as long as they didn't take up a whole day of my life, I did everything alone. And while it took a great deal of getting used to, I became comfortable with that reality.

So, when Dane said I'm not doing it alone, it made me realize just how detached I was from life as I once knew it.

"You, okay?" He caught me daydreaming.

"Yeah, just got a little distracted." I shook my head.

"Can you pass me another roll?" He peered down at the pile beside my feet.

"Sure." I smiled as I passed him another roll of wallpaper.

"Any plans for the weekend?" Dane asked.

"Yeah, I was going to take the kayak out before the lake freezes over." I replied.

"That sounds fun." He nodded his head with his face still to the wall and he stuck down wallpaper.

"Yeah, Tux loves being on the water. It's our thing." I said.

"That's sweet. I bet he loves those days." Dane replied.

"It's always a bath after for both of us, but a good time." I smiled as Tux came in and rubbed my side as he yawned.

"Where will you go? If you don't mind me asking." He said sheepishly.

"Anywhere I don't have to drag a double kayak too far, or too steep." I laughed.

"Want us to come and give you a hand while you find somewhere you're comfortable with? I was thinking of taking the girls for a picnic somewhere before the weather starts to turn." He was still giving off uncertainty in his tone.

"I'd love it if you guys came along. Maybe the girls would like a turn on the kayak just in the shallow water?" I asked.

"That sounds great. I know they'd love to give it a try. They're on sale at the moment, if they like it enough, we might have to pick some up." He turned back to me and smiled.

"It's a good hobby, keeps them outside and off the devices." I chuckled.

"Picnic? What are you making us for lunch?" I giggled.

"Anything you want from the Toastie shop. It's on the way to the yacht club, great views of all the houses with their own docks." He suggested.

"That sounds absolutely perfect, even if you were teasing about the toasties." I smiled.

"Well good, I wasn't teasing." Dane laughed.

I continued to hand him roll after roll of wallpaper and soon we were moving onto Cassie's room.

As I looked around the paint was still a little patchy and would need a second coat. I examined each wall thoroughly and Dane grabbed a paintbrush.

"No, you've already showered. Let me tackle this one tomorrow. Audrey's room should be good to go if you're up for another room of wallpapering." I sighed.

"Sure thing." He headed to Audrey's room and brought the huge spotlight with him.

The room was cold from the open windows, and he shut them and drew the blinds over the wide window.

"I was thinking a reading nook, cushion bench, and a bookshelf in the sides of the walls and some dim lighting." I explained as I started pointing out my thoughts.

"Furry cushions and blankets." He smiled as he looked at the area and began to visualize. "Maybe some festoon lights or fairy lights." He hummed.

"We could build the bench seat with some storage drawers for some extra blankets." I added.

"She would love that." He agreed.

"Let's get to wallpapering." I sighed.

"You must be tired. Why don't you get some sleep, this shouldn't take me too long." Dane brushed my hair back behind my ear.

The touch of him sent a jolt of heat through my body and I'd longed for his body to be pressed against mine again. Every moment felt too long to wait, and I reached for his neck and pulled his lips into mine.

His hands moved down my body and tangled in my hair as I pulled at his singlet, all the while his lips were holding onto mine.

"Stella." He pulled back and whispered softly.

"Yess…" I purred.

"Come upstairs." He grasped my hand and pulled me up the stairs to the big open room.

"This can be yours if you want." He walked me around with my hand in his as he showed me the bathroom and a walk-in closet. This seemed to have been intended as a master bedroom.

"Why don't you take this room, it's so much bigger than yours?" I asked.

"I like to be on the same floor as the girls." He confessed with his protective dad's voice. "And it has everything you will need for privacy and for Tux. Storage if you want to bring things inside when the snow comes in. Winters here are rough." He smiled.

"So, you want me to move in?" I laughed.

"Not move in, just fill up the empty space for a while." He laughed back with a hint of embarrassment.

"Let me think about it?" I winked.

"No pressure, you are welcome to live under feet upon feet of snow if you want to." He teased.

"You'd come and rescue me, wouldn't you?" I pressed as I squinted my eyes at him.

"If I could get to you, you might turn into an icy pole out there. We'd never hear you scream under all that powder." He whispered playfully.

"Hmmm...Tux what do you say?" I knelt to Tux and played with his floppy ears.

"If I know Tux, he's already moved in." Dane laughed.

I walked around the room as I seriously began to consider the idea and smiled when I poked my head into the huge bathroom.

"Why wouldn't you use this as an office?" I asked.

"I still can, if you're open to getting a room divider." He replied.

"Can we get a double bench?" I asked.

"Sure, you're building it though." He grinned.

"Fine, I suppose you need me. I'll save you Dane the damsel in distress." I teased. "But you should ask the girls first if they are comfortable with this." I suggested.

"No need, it was their idea." He confessed.

"You totally rank at the bottom of the ladder in this hierarchy." I laughed.

"I just pay the bills and pick up the takeout." He smiled.

"I think you're doing a great job." I brushed his hand with my little finger.

Dane pulled me by that finger and reached his arms around my waist and pulled me closer to him and I matched his embrace with my arms resting on his shoulder blades.

"I'm scared we'll ruin a good thing…" I sighed.

"Can only get better, right?" He asked.

"I'm not here, for forever. I want to be able to come back here one day and pick up where we left off. I want us to be friends, but I also can't wait to see how you use that thing in your pants." I choked with unexpected honesty.

"Stella, I'm not ready for anything and clearly you aren't either and we can have this conversation over and over until we are blue in the face and balls. Or we can embrace the moment and just live." He stroked my cheek with the back of his hand, and I brushed through his beard softly.

I held my index finger up in front of our faces indicating *one.* He kissed my finger, each lip slightly wrapped around it so he could taste me. I reached my arms around his neck, and he lifted me up into him cupping my ass as I wrestled with his clothing. He placed me down on the floor as he climbed over me, he removed my underwear and I pulled at him until he was free and ready for me.

"Dane…" I gasped as he kissed my inner thighs and primed me with his fingers. Slowly plunging them into me. My hands tangled in his hair as I pulled him into me with a hint of aggression. He began to circle my clit with his tongue as he experimented with an extra finger now and soon, I was ready to climax.

"No, wait for me." He climbed off of me.

I pushed him to the ground and climbed on top of him and secured myself onto him and I rocked back and forth slowly squeezing my muscles to suck him in as deep as he could fit, his girth filling me just right. It was so deep it might hurt but he was a gentle lover and paid close attention to my body and all its cues.

He sat up with me, we were face to face and this was soon becoming the best sex I've ever had. I wanted to feel his length inside me, and I bounced up and down and he held my thighs as they shook over him guarding me from going too deep.

"Oh. My. God. I think I'm going to cum." His eyes began to roll back, and I rested over him so deep inside me and I rocked back and forth with a greedy hunger for him to fill me up with every drop of him. I bucked back and forth and soon it sent us both over the edge into a pile of sweaty hormones. He rolled me over and pounded me harder while he was still erect sending my orgasm into overdrive, I squirmed in a full-body spasm as he made me cum a second time, this time so much harder and I collapsed onto the floor like a ragdoll.

I wasn't sure what liquids were on me, sweat, cum, her sweet pussy nectar. I hoped for all three and I wanted this every day for the rest of my life.

I slumped onto the floor beside her and turned to face her. Her eyes closed, lips plump and she wore a sweetly satisfied smile. I stroked her cheek and played with her hair as she moved a little closer to me. I wrapped my arms around her, and she accepted willingly as she pressed her body into him and rested her head into the nook of my arm and chest.

She ran her hand over my chest, exaggerating every mound that resembled muscle.

"Stop it." I laughed grabbing her hand gently and holding it against my chest.

"How do you find time to work out." She asked.

"I don't anymore, Lilly always wants to be carried though, and then there's yard work. Guess all the little things help." I said.

"Guess so." She rubbed my chest gently. "We should get some sleep." She yawned.

"Not yet…If I only get one night…" I pointed my finger at her and bopped her nose with it.

We didn't have to say anything, I think we just knew how good it felt to be held by another person. How good it felt to know this person in my arms wasn't responsible for any unhappiness in my life. She had enriched my life beyond measure in such a short burst of time. I also knew I couldn't be greedy with her. She wanted to grow, to stretch her wings.

My daughters wanted her too, to braid their hair, make their costumes, and dance till their feet hurt cause that's what distracted them from the absence of Gina.

Gina wasn't a bad mother; she just wasn't mother material. She had become a terrible wife and that was because I had been an absent husband. By the time I got the chance at a normal lifestyle the damage had been done, I had missed too much, and she found someone else to fill in the blanks.

Stella's hand pulled at my cheek, and I turned to face her.

"Penny for your thoughts?" she whispered.

"You don't wanna know." I smiled as I pulled her tightly into me as if I couldn't be close enough to her.

"How about a shower?" She propped herself up.

"Yeah, we probably should. It's picnic day tomorrow." I yawned.

"It is!" She smiled.

Stella stood up, pulled her clothes back on, descended the staircase, and headed for the bathroom. I collected two towels from the laundry and carried them in while she ran the hot water.

"Are you coming in?" she poked her head around the curtain.

As steam billowed out from behind her, I recoiled in fear.

"That's too hot for me." I laughed.

"Pussy…" She snickered and shut the curtain.

I could see the silhouette of her naked body as she shampooed her hair and lathered her breasts with body wash, and I dropped my clothes instantly to brave the heat for one last intimate moment with her. After all, we had agreed to one night only.

"Fancy seeing you here, she wrapped her arms around my neck and her body was hot to the touch.

"Phwoar! Can we turn the heat down just a little? A shower shouldn't result in second-degree burns." I reached for the nozzle.

"But I'll get cold." She pouted.

"I'll keep you warm." I kissed her pink lips. "We did say one whole night." I washed the shampoo from the ends of her hair.

"Do you wanna sleep in the van with me?" She asked.

"Hmm, it's Saturday tomorrow. The girls will be up early to film their cereal video. We could pull out Audrey's mattress and bunk in the lounge room?" I suggested.

"I'm in." She agreed.

She finished first and wrapped herself in a towel while I finished in the shower, I had finally been able to temper it lower.

Stella was out on the back patio brushing off Audrey's mattress and trying to pull it in alone.

"Wait!" I whispered loudly.

"Shhhhhh!" She hushed me.

Tux was jumping at the mattress excitedly trying to help Stella and I began to pull from the front end. After a few hefty drags, we were finally in the lounge room, and we dropped the mattress down on the carpet in front of the couch.

I walked into my room and gathered some spare pillows and blankets from open unsorted boxes. Stella met me at the door and took them from me as she motioned with her chin that Lilly was uncovered and needed to be tucked back in. Audrey was a classic blanket hog and would wrap herself in the blanket like a snake. Even more so when they were mink or fluffy blankets. Cassie would kick off every blanket no matter what the temperature was, and I had made a habit of making sure she was dressed appropriately for bed depending on the weather just to be safe.

When I walked out Stella was snuggly wrapped in a blanket. I climbed in beside her and with a second blanket and cozied myself in with her.

"Goodnight." She yawned with her eyes closed.

I leaned over and kissed her forehead gently and she pulled in a little closer to me and I wrapped an arm around her as she tucked a leg between my legs.

The sun peeked through the blinds viciously ready to disturb the short sleep I'd had. But that wasn't what alarmed me. It was the girls giggling in the kitchen riffling through cereal boxes in search of their next victim and the fact that they might have seen Stella and I entwined in our sleep.

"Shut up, Cassie. You big mouth!" Audrey hissed as I felt eyes on me.

"They look so comfy! I hope I get to cuddle a boy like that when I'm older." Lilly chuckled.

"You'll be married and over thirty when that happens." I pulled myself up and stretched.

Stella wriggled away and found a new victim in a pillow as she fought for just a few more minutes of sleep.

"Why were you snuggling Stella, Daddy?" Lilly asked.

"She was cold. You guys took all the blankets!" I tried to push blame playfully.

"Oh! Sorry." Audrey bit her bottom lip as if she knew I meant her.

"It's okay, we just got tired after wallpapering the rooms and we crashed in here." I pulled myself up and walked to the kitchen.

"I need to teach one of you how to make coffee if you're going to keep getting up before me." I eyeballed Cassie knowing she'd be the most reliable, but also the most likely to drink it and like it.

"I'll learn." Cassie beamed as if she knew I was thinking of her.

I boiled the kettle first then pulled out a clean paper filter and placed it in the machine, wet it, filled it with ground coffee, and poured in hot water from the kettle.

"Woah, I know what to get you for Christmas." Stella laughed as she sat next to Lilly at the bench. Lilly was watching me intent on learning this like it was a survival skill.

"What will you buy him?" Lilly asked.

"A Nespresso machine! This here is an ancient way of making coffee. People my age use pods." She winked.

"It's fine!" I laughed. "I happen to like this way." I rolled my eyes playfully.

"But maybe if there's two of you drinking it you should get one bigger." Audrey acknowledged the size of the pot.

"Well, they do a mini version. It's cute and compact and will spare you any spills." I suggested.

"But mini?" Lilly poked.

"I won't be here forever Lil." Stella sighed as she rubbed Lilly's back.

"Why not? Dad needs you." She sulked.

Stella's smile turned upside down as she tried to comfort Lilly and say all the right things.

But Lilly was right. I needed Stella a lot more than she needed me.

Stella's phone rang and she ran to answer it. While she was gone, I took the chance to whisper between me and the girls.

"Girls, Stella can't stay here forever. She's got plans and a life of her own she needs to enjoy. We are helping her by letting her stay here and that's why she's helping us in return.' I tried to explain.

"You and mom *never* cuddled like that." Audrey gawked at me with her eyebrows expressively furrowed.

I was a little speechless but tried to compose myself instead of making any expressions that could throw me under the bus.

"We don't care, we like Stella!" Cassie exclaimed loudly.

"Cuddle her more so she stays." Lilly shook her finger at me.

"No, that would be selfish of us." I sighed.

"Fine, leave it up to us then." Cassie placed her elbows on the bench and extended her hands open and the other two granted her the downward high five she commanded.

"You guys are scary!" I backed away as I laughed and shook my head.

"Dad, grab that Japanese cereal. You'll need to translate it with that app." Audrey requested.

"STELLA!" Cassie beckoned her.

Stella popped her head out of a room still on the phone and said goodbye and walked over towards us hanging up the phone.

"Cass…"I scolded.

"No, I was hanging up anyway. Just my mom, she's being difficult. Cassie, it's like you could sense I needed saving. Good work!" Stella high-fived her.

"I'm the only one not getting one of those today." I glowered a little jealous.

"Well do as you're told, and you might still get one." Lilly flicked her hair dramatically.

I tried to ignore her as I grabbed the cereal and gave the girls my phone so they could translate it themselves and set up an area to film their video.

"Everything okay with your mom?" I asked Stella.

"Yeah. She just thought I was going to get an apartment here. She booked tickets to come out for a visit." She explained.

"She can stay here!" I offered with excitement for her.

"No, it's my dad too. It's too much to ask of you. If they insist, I'll tell them to get a hotel." She smiled.

"That sounds expensive. We have plenty of room here, the girls can share a room. Look, we'll figure it out. Call her back." I pressed.

"Dane…" She said with a deep breath.

"Do as you're told!" I grabbed her phone and dialed her mom.

"Take your own advice!" Cassie glowered at me with her intense eyes.

"What is going on right now?" Stella snapped her head in the direction of the girls with confusion as Lilly enthusiastically hugged Audrey, but Audrey pushed her off like she was a germ.

"Hi, Stella's mom?" I walked away with the phone.

"Yes, you must be Dane?" She replied. She had a bubbly warm voice.

"You're welcome to come stay here, no need to cancel anything." By now Stella was trying to wrestle the phone from my hands, but I was much bigger than her and all her attempts failed, I shook her off of me every time.

"DANE!" She shouted at me.

"Tell Stella I'll email her our itinerary. We look forward to meeting you and the girls." I could feel her genuine smile through the phone, and I bid her farewell and hung up the phone. Stella was sat cross-legged on the floor with her arms crossed across her chest and a disappointed look on her face like a sulky teenager.

"You idiot!" She laughed.

"You'll thank me when you get to hug your mom." I sighed.

"I haven't seen her since I left home…" She confessed.

"That's a while then." I kneeled to her level.

She jumped up without making eye contact and she watched the girls as they started filming their video. Each one tried the new cereal and reacted and then they pulled Stella in to view and made her try the cereal with them.

"Hi, guys! This is Stella. She's our live-in nanny! She is going to be popping into videos too!" Cassie explained.

"Hi everyone!" Stella waved at the camera and took a bite of the cereal, first dry and then with milk and described the taste and texture and gave it a rating out of ten.

Finally, they wrapped up the video and I could speak without being scolded or given the filthy looks girls give when they want to tell you what to do without words.

"Okay get ready, pack some bathers, towels, and a change of clothes." I ordered.

"Where are we going?" Audrey asked.

"Stella is taking Tux for a kayak. We're going to join them for a picnic. We'll pick up some toasties from that toasty shop." I explained.

"YES!" Cassie squealed with excitement.

Before I could reply they had all run off to the laundry dumped out their school bags and began filling them with all the items I had suggested.

"Done! Let's go." Lilly popped up in front of me with a half-zipped bag that overflowed and was half her size and I couldn't help but laugh.

"Give me that bag, you can go help Stella and Tux." I bent down and begged for a high five with my hand up.

Lilly looked at me and then my hand and gave me a gentle slap and then proceeded with a big hug.

"Don't tell Cassie." She kissed my cheek loudly.

"Our secret." I rubbed her back and gave her a gentle squeeze.

Lilly trotted off towards the front door and disappeared out the front where Tux was waiting for her. I unpacked her bag, folded the contents properly, and removed anything unnecessary like the snow boots she had snuck in.

Cassie and Audrey were dressed in their bathers with shirts pulled over, each with sunglasses and hats on.

"Good…" I smiled at them. "Any contraband in those?" I held up Lilly's snow boots.

"Dad, we know to pack flip flops…" Audrey rolled her eyes playfully as she took the boots from me and tossed them into my room.

"Hey! That's my room." I grumbled.

"It's our room till you and Stella finish *our* rooms." She smiled.

"Maybe even until you finish our costumes…" Cassie added smugly.

"Oh! I like that. Let's do that." Audrey high-fived her.

"Are you kidding me?" I stepped back in defeat. "I'll work on the rooms tonight." I threw my hands up in defense.

"Don't forget the mattresses." Cassie added.

"Fuck!" I pressed my hand to my forehead.

"HEY! That's a dollar." Audrey shook her index finger at me like I was a child.

"Oh, take five! That'll cover me for the weekend." I held out the only Lincoln bill I had in my wallet.

"Thank you!" Cassie plucked the note from my hand and placed it in the jar on top of the fridge.

I shooed the girls outside and locked the door behind me and Stella was dressed in a swimming tank and shorts. She had a wet bag packed with some extras and Tux was harnessed and wearing a life jacket.

"Do you wanna go together? We can strap the kayak to the roof racks.

"If you think there's enough room in the back for Tux we can." She nodded.

"Easily." I opened the doors for Tux then went to her van, unstrapped the kayak, and brought it over to the truck.

"Seriously! I've never been able to lift this thing alone or drag it without the wheel and you pick it up like it's a tic tac." Stella scowled.

"Hey, he's an ex-SEAL. He's a qualified diver too. Stick around…" Cassie smirked.

Stella laughed awkwardly as she jumped onto the sidestep of the truck and did the straps to secure the kayak down.

"So subtle." She whispered across the roof of the truck.

"No fear, *none*! It's problematic." I laughed.

"I'm not problematic!" Cassie slapped my leg.

"Hey! No hitting." I jumped down and pushed their bags into the trunk.

Tux was a big heavy dog and he seemed to need some help getting into the truck, he paced impatiently between the truck and the van with eyes glued to the kayak.

"Come on buddy." I called.

He came right away, and I placed his front paws on the back of the truck, lifted his back legs, and helped him in. He turned to me and licked my hand as a thank you and I patted him as I checked his vest was secure enough.

"Okay, I think that's everything." Stella said as she jumped down from the truck and handed me a cooler with drinks.

"Let's go!" I jumped into the driver's side and Stella beside me.

I could feel Cassie's eyes burning the back of my head with her mischievous grin as she plotted our future. Cassie had that wild imagination and it often let her down. She was my dreamer, the one with the larger-than-life plans. Something I'd only recently learned about her.

Between being away for weeks or months quite often and having two other kids on either side of her, Cassie and I missed out on bonding. Sure, I was there for night feeds on the odd occasion, but we never bonded. Even though I could *feel* her love so irrefutably, I didn't deserve the protection she gave me. Cassie was fiercer than the others, she wasn't afraid to go after all the things she wanted in life. She wasn't afraid to make her own path and follow it to the end.

Audrey suffered from my neglect of my family the longest, and I think that was a big contributor to why she became such a bookworm. She was always off escaping to a faraway land in the depths of her pages where things were a little safer and more consistent, she got to control when the book closed. She didn't have that control at home. Audrey was the nurturer; she was amazing with Lilly and had a lot of time for Cassie's wild ideas, but it came at a cost. She became too mature too fast to the point where she was often telling me how to do things.

Lilly was too young to understand the depth of what had happened. She knew her mother was gone, but not the reason why. She was so distracted by the move that she hadn't stopped to ask questions. She hadn't found time to miss Gina, but I knew eventually she would.

As we drove to Toasty the girls sang along to their current favorite song as Tux perched his head between the headrests. Stella had a baseball cap on with dark sunglasses and looked somewhat disheveled.

"Are you okay?" I whispered.

"I'm good." She sniffed as we pulled into the parking lot of Toasty's.

Stella leaped out of the truck first and walked a little faster than usual to the shop. The girls and I rushed to catch up.

"Hungry?" I asked over her shoulder.

"Famished." She said softly as she scanned the menu.

"I'll have a grilled cheese please." Lilly tugged at my arm.

"Hawaiian for me." Audrey added.

"I'll have a Turkey please." Cassie smiled.

"A live one?" I joked.

She glared at me and scoffed at my unappreciated banter, and I shook my head. I'd have to work on jokes with her.

"I'll grab a bacon burger." I followed up with the cashier.

"Make that two please." Stella stepped forward and paid for all our meals.

"You didn't have to do that; I was going to get it." I tugged her elbow softly.

"I wanted to." She said through her dark glasses.

"What's wrong Stella? You're off all of a sudden." I asked as I pulled her away from the girls who were sitting at a table with cans of root beer, we had packed.

Stella stared out the window of the shop at Tux who had his head out the window ready to say hi to anyone who passed him.

"I promise I'm fine. Just feeling a little bleurgh." She lied.

"Sick? I can take you home?" I pressed.

"I'm not sick." She walked to the counter to collect Lilly's order and placed it in front of her as she sat down with the girls to avoid me.

Stella

He wasn't wrong and his senses were sending my stomach into overdrive with backflips.

The truth was I was never okay on a kayaking day. As many as I'd had over the years, and as much as I wanted it. Kayaking was a mourning for me. I saw Ana in every single body of water I entered. We grew up together, on the water, in that very kayak. As kids, we were on the water more than we were on the land in the summer. That kayak housed all my joy, gossip, and grief. It was the only part of Ana I had left. It was all I wanted; it was where I felt the most connected and where I could feel her presence. Even after all the years that had gone by, nothing felt right.

But something about today felt harder and keeping my glasses down was all I could do to stop my eyes from pooling with unwelcome tears.

There was something about this family that made me feel like I was missing out on something more. Life on the road was just a really good way to hide from therapists.

Maybe it was the part about my parents coming to town that was agitating me.

The last time I saw them I told my mom I'd call every day. She was lucky if I called once a month. She even asked for the feed to my campervan surveillance just so she could check in when I wasn't answering my phone cause she knew I was just being a hermit and staring at the screen as it rang.

In truth, I had crawled so deeply within my shell of mourning that all the entrances to me had shrunk beneath a dark veil. It was getting harder to see and feel good. That instantly changed when I met Dane and his girls. They peeled back the heavy layers and a part of me I didn't know still existed came out because I knew they needed me more than *I* needed me.

I was having fun with the girls, they liked me, and I was doing things that someone else found useful. I sang and danced for the first time in a long time without alcoholic influences and I shared my body with this man who made me feel like he would worship me.

If reality was anything to go off, I should be floating on a fluffy cloud sipping a martini like a cherub, life could be that sweet and indulgent, but of course, I wasn't going to let it.

I felt Dane's arm brush past me as he placed plates of food down in front of me and the girls. A massive burger with cheesy patties and crispy bacon. I wasn't lying when I said I was famished. I craved something I hadn't cooked and something that didn't come in a box or plastic container. It was incredible to have something so fresh and I didn't feel an ounce of regret about how greasy it was.

Dane came back with his food next and finally sat across from me and ate his food without making any eye contact with me. The girls chattered amongst themselves as they ate their chips and almost cold toasties.

"Okay, let's get some sandwiches for later and head off." Dane said.

The girls stood up and headed to a fridge with a freshly made sandwich selection and small platters of fruit and cheese with cold cuts of fresh deli meats.

One by one the girls piled the food into Dane's arms, and they all headed back to the car while I waited for Dane.

He handed me one of the bags of food and with his free arm pressed his hand to my back to comfort me.

"If it's about last night, I'm sorry. It won't happen again." He apologized.

"No, it's not that. It's not you, it's me." I said under my breath. "This is what I do to cope, I thought I'd be okay, I've been doing it long enough…" I sighed.

"I can drop you off if you want, give you some space?" He said reassuringly.

"No, I don't want the girls to think I'm upset with them being with me. Let's just go, I'll paddle out for a bit till I can pull myself together." I nodded my head.

"You're sure?" He asked.

"Absolutely." I replied.

"Do you need a hug?" He asked.

"NO! Do not hug a girl who's emotional, that's an invitation for a waterfall." I laughed.

"Okay, glad it wasn't the us thing." He smiled.

"There's no us thing Dane. There's you and the girls, and then there's me. Let's not complicate it." I tried to sound kind, but he knew the deal.

"Sorry, I didn't mean that. Okay…deep breath, just friends." He laughed it off.

"It's not you, you're perfect. I'm just emotionally unavailable." I sighed.

"You're not so good at letting a guy down easy." He rubbed his forehead with a sarcastic tone in his voice.

"Yeah, I'll shut up now. Shall we?" I pointed to the truck.

"YES!" Dane said as he rushed to the truck.

I was scolding myself inside, I had well and truly fucked any chances of sex again. And I had come across as a self-entitled bitch who thought she could call all the shots from having a meltdown.

When we arrived at the yacht club Dane helped me unstrap the kayak and I pulled it over to the bank. Dane and the girls went to hire two double kayaks so they could all paddle together.

Once I had my vest on and my oar screwed into one whole length, I called Tux into the front of the kayak, and I climbed in after him. I paddled out as fast as I could and tried to put a good amount of distance between myself and the others while I pretended to study the coast and birds. Once I was far enough away Tux turned around slowly and laid down, now he was facing me. He let out a sigh knowing what was about to follow. I pulled my oar in, and I stretched back and screamed. I screamed because life had been so unfair. Soulmates aren't always lovers, they can be a friend, a relative, or a stranger, and it's completely platonic. Ana was that for me. I walked through life constantly questioning the *what-ifs.*

They say grief gets easier, that it makes you stronger. I don't feel stronger. I feel empty, I feel like there's a piece of me missing, water filled those holes so easily and healed me if only for a short time until the holes opened back up again.

I never stopped hating my phone, the ringtone, and the words that followed after I said *hello…* it was the irony of it being our main form of connection and also the thing that delivered the news with gravity I couldn't even comprehend. Maybe that's why I was so detached from it, why I didn't answer my parents' phone calls.

The firsts were the worst. The first Christmas we wouldn't exchange gifts, my first birthday without her, her birthday, even though she wouldn't age anymore. There were so many new ways I needed to experience life all over again because I was alone now. Without her, alone was all that felt acceptable. I found grief to be relentless, and at times like now, it becomes an overwhelming pain that makes you physically unwell. Tux always knows this point. He places his giant paw on my ankle and reminds me I'm not without a friend. There were a lot of band-aid solutions, shopping, working, and TV. And they were fine, life does indeed go on, but it doesn't stop the feelings from coming in sometimes.

I guess that's why I kept busy by taking on the extra work.

At Dane's, it felt like a safe haven for the hours I had spare. The girls had so much spark that they made *me* feel a little glittery around them, my mind was occupied, there was no time to think outside of them and I was happier because of it.

I wept a little longer today. I pulled my knees to my chest, and I breathed through the pain as I relived that day at an express speed. Then I splashed my face with water, picked my oar back up, and carried on trying to enjoy the day like I knew she would want me to.

Cassie and Audrey were picking up speed as they finally learned to work together and in unison to steer the kayak.

Dane and Lilly hung back a little as Lilly scooped at the water with a pond net trying to catch something.

"STELLA!" Cassie yelled.

I stayed still and waited for the girls to come to me as I waved at them.

It wasn't long and they took some time to slow down as they caught up with me.

"Slow down girls." I used my oar to try and block them from colliding with me.

"SHIT!" Audrey screamed.

I lunged at their kayak trying to stop it from overturning, but my weight did little to help. They tipped over in what felt like slow motion and soon they were under the kayak.

I was already in the water and luckily the girls had life vests on, so they quickly popped up giggling.

I grabbed the kayak and flipped it as I helped Cassie try to climb back in.

Tux leaped into the water to help, and he went for Audrey and dragged her towards me. She seemed to be a weaker swimmer than Cassie and shivered in the water as I hauled her up into the kayak.

Dane and Lilly were chasing my kayak now and collected my loose oar from the water.

"Everyone okay?" He asked as he held the kayak still for Tux to climb back in as I pushed him up from behind.

Tux was a huge dog and extremely heavy, heavier still when he was wet, and it took all my strength to push him in.

He shook off the water as he settled back into his spot, and I used the rest of my energy to pull myself up and into the kayak.

"Phew, everyone okay?" I said as I caught my breath.

"That was awesome!" Cassie exacerbated.

"Let's not do that again." I puffed with exhaustion.

Dane hurled a bottle of water onto my kayak, and I poured some water into my hand for Tux, and he slurped up the water as I let it flow freely over my hand as he drank.

"You guys still up for a lap? Maybe down to that big tree and back." I smiled.

"Race you there!" Cassie began paddling and Audrey rolled her eyes as she slowly joined Cassie.

Audrey was so much more of an introvert but did her best to join in with group activities.

Dane and Lilly were already underway, and I did my best to catch up, but I had a little extra weight that didn't paddle in my bear-like companion, slash lifeguard.

"Come on!" Dane turned back and laughed as I lagged behind.

"No fair, you have a helper." I grumbled.

Cassie and Audrey were now on their returning lap and Dane ordered them to follow back with us as a group in case they flipped again.

"Seriously, I'm not paddling." Audrey grouched as she crossed her arms.

"Dad, we should be home finishing our rooms and making costumes." Lilly agreed with Audrey.

"That's what I get for letting their mother buy them iPads at such a young age." Dane sighed.

"It's okay, it is quite cold out here." I assured him I wasn't offended.

"Who wants to help wash Tux?" I asked the girls as we paddled back to the truck.

"Oh! ME." Audrey was very much an animal person and she had taken well to Tux, and he was equally just as fond of her.

We finally hit the landing and Dane dragged their kayaks back to the clubhouse as I dried myself off with a towel and helped the girls do the same.

Dane walked around the other side of the truck and he was drying off Tux, hugging him and thanking him for helping Audrey.

"You might just be the best dog I've ever met." He whispered as he fed him the remainder of his burger.

Tux was always more than willing to eat any food offered to him, and he gobbled it down in two, maybe even one bite.

Dane lifted the kayak onto the roof, and I jumped onto the step to help secure it while the girls ate ice creams on the grass as they dried off a little better in the sun.

"Are you okay?" Dane whispered over the roof.

"Mhmm." I tried not to speak.

He looked at me longingly but with sympathetic eyes, not lustrous.

I covered my seat with a towel and climbed into the truck and fixed my hair while I waited for the girls to finish and soon enough, they bounded over and into the truck ready to go home.

We pulled into the driveway and Audrey ran to my van waiting for all the instructions on how to wash such a woolly dog.

"I'm so excited." She beamed.

"He's going to love the extra massages." I smiled.

I went into the van and Audrey followed and I handed her a plastic storage container of hairbrushes, shampoo, nail clippers, treats, and scissors.

"Woah!" She peeked into the box.

"Yeah, Tux needs a few different types of hairbrushes, he has what is called a double coat." I explained. "He's also got a water-resistant coat and webbed feet. Not too many dogs have that." I smiled.

"Audrey was a sponge for information and drank in everything I told her about Tux.

She walked him off with the large expandable tub I handed her that he barely fit in towards the side of the house where there was water access.

"You know, I had no idea she even liked animals, now she wants to be a pet groomer." Dane stood beside me and sighed.

"Maybe you should get her a pet, it would bring her out of her shell a little." I suggested.

"Another dog?" He asked.

"Maybe a cat, she's a book girl, the right cat would cuddle with her for hours and it would help her resign the role of nurturing her sisters to make time for the kitten." I said.

"You think?" Dane asked.

"I think the separation was hardest on her. She feels the need to fill that spot, something else a little smaller that needs the same TLC might help her back away and be a kid a little more." I pondered.

"A cat you reckon?" Dane stroked his beard.

"A ragdoll is docile, super lazy. She could probably even dress it up." I softly hit him on the bicep.

"I'll think about it…" He smiled as I walked to follow Audrey.

She already had Tux in the tub with a good amount of warm water and I poured a heap of shampoo all over his fur and we began scrubbing gently at his fur and he loved every moment of it.

Once we needed to wash off the suds, I collapsed the bucket flat to let the water out easier and we hosed him off before we added a treatment and conditioner to help soften his fur.

"Can I do his tail?" Audrey asked.

"Of course." I poured some conditioner into her hands, and she brushed it softly through the length of his tail.

"Do you want to rinse him?" I held out the hose for her.

"YES!" She smiled.

She reached for the hose and ran the water over him till he was fresh and clean. Dane brought out some old towels to dry him and a hairdryer.

"Now the fun part." I sighed as I glared at the box of hairbrushes.

"Tell me which one, I'll do it." She said enthusiastically.

"Those ones." I pointed to the undercoat and slicker brushes.

"They help to detangle and remove any loose hair." I explained as I showed her how to brush through the different parts of his hair.

Tux was dry and looked immaculate. All we needed to do was trim his nails. Audrey watched as I sniped away at the length of his claws and trimmed his paw pad hair on his feet.

"Tux, you look so pretty!" Audrey kissed his big snout.

"You on the other hand could use a shower." Dane laughed as he plucked off fistfuls of Tux's hair from her shoulder.

"Okay." She sighed and led Tux into the house with a jerky treat.

"You stink." Dane squirted the hose at me.

"Hey!" I chased him with a wet towel to whip him.

"Not fair!" He froze and held his arms up.

The clouds over us began to darken fast and soon enough it would rain. Dane ordered me inside and he took over to rinse out the collapsible tub and turned off the water for me.

Dane

The girls were rustling through an empty pantry and a sparser fridge when I came in and they complained they were hungry.

"Can we order in?" Audrey begged.

"NO, we've eaten way too much takeout since we moved here." I said bravely.

"Well…father. There's nothing to cook, even Stella agreed so she's gone to fight the monstrosity of laundry once more, she also said you need to put your clothes away!" Cassie said sternly.

I was never going to win a fight against this kid. She was so much bossier than I remember but she also had wit and a serious ability to get her way.

"Fine, Burger King. We'll shop after." I slumped onto a bar stool.

"Nice!" Lilly high-fived Cassie like they'd won a victory.

"When did you guys get so old…" I sighed.

"We aren't that old, dad." Audrey grunted as she poured out a carton of expired milk down the sink.

"You are!" I said as I watched her clean out the fridge of odd bits and pieces that were too old to use.

"Cassie. Write a list." I pushed over a pad and pen.

"Goldfish!" Lilly shouted.

"Mac and Cheese." Audrey added.

"Pancake mix." I shook an empty box that had been placed in the pantry.

"Oops…" Lilly covered her mouth and giggled.

"In her defense, it's not all gone. She poured it into a bowl. See…" Audrey placed the bowl down on the bench beside me as she protected her little sister.

"Okay, wise! I'll give you that one Lil." I laughed.

"Can we have those giant nuggets again?" Cassie asked.

"Oh, the ones Stella makes?" Audrey's eyes lit up.

"YES! STELLA." Lilly yelled.

"Hi?" Stella poked her head around the corner with a pile of socks in her arms.

"What do we need for those big nuggets you made?" Cassie asked.

"Ummmm, chicken breast, Napolitana sauce, cheese, panko breadcrumbs, milk, eggs. I think that's it." She wrinkled her nose as she revised the list she'd given Cassie.

"OH! And a meat mallet would be awesome." She finished as she disappeared back down the hallway.

"Lasagna?" I added.

"Really..." Cassie rolled her eyes at me.

"What, I need to eat too. This isn't the Audrey, Cassie and Lilly list." I grunted.

"Fine, what else?" Lilly smiled.

"Bacon, milk, eggs, butter, bread, steak, sausage meat, hotdogs..." Cassie cut me off with her hand held in my face.

"STOP. You gotta write this. I'm still at eggs." Her eyes widened as she passed me the pad and ran off to the TV.

"Useless..." I laughed.

"That's not very nice." Lilly shook her head at me as she banged the pancake carton on the bench one more time.

"I was just joking." I replied a little scared of Lilly's seriousness.

Lilly tugged at my arm and pulled my eye to her lips. "Can we get ice cream?" she whispered. Her eyes were now bulging, and they horrified me.

I picked her up and placed her on the bench.

"Of course, we can baby girl." I kissed her hand, and she gave me the big hug I really needed after going up against the older girls.

"Maybe some chocolate sauce and sprinkles?" She fluttered her eyelashes.

I nodded as I laughed and instructed her to go and play with her sisters and Tux while I finished the list. Stella walked past us and headed for one of the bedrooms that still needed another coat of paint.

"Stella?" I knocked on the door and smelt a fresh coat of paint going on the wall.

"Yes?" She answered.

"Need anything from the store?" I asked.

"Actually, I need an emergency contraceptive." She whispered.

"Oh shit, I'm sorry about that." I sighed.

"No, it's cool. I just don't want to risk it." She replied.

"I get that. Why don't we go tonight then after we feed these kids and get groceries? They can pick out their new beds so we can have them delivered next week too." I suggested.

"Sounds good. I think these rooms are done now. Could use some nice rugs, I grabbed a bunch of décors already." She smiled as she took a lap of Cassie's room.

"Go shower." I ordered.

"Yes, boss." She giggled.

"I'm not your boss." I laughed.

"Sometimes you are." She added.

"Not here, we're housemates with benefits." I winked.

"Benefits?" she queried.

"Yeah, like how you do our laundry and I let your dog run in my yard." I shrugged.

She threw a dry brush at me and pushed me playfully out of the room, and I wanted to pick her up and kiss her. But I didn't, I couldn't.

Stella brushed past me as she walked to the shower and the girls put on raincoats.

I added more items to the list and folded it and placed it in my pant pocket.

Soon Stella was ready, and she wore black sweatpants and a grey hoodie and had a nightmare before Christmas umbrella tucked under her arm.

"See you soon Tux." She bent down and hugged him.

We piled into the truck, headed to Burger King, and dined in.

"I'll have a bacon king." Cassie said to the cashier.

"Cheeseburger, please. Hold the pickles." Lilly smiled.

"Chicken nuggets for me." Audrey added.

"Double Texas please." I added.

"Stella?" I called her over.

"I'm not sure yet, you go ahead and finish up." She turned back to the menu and scanned for options.

I knew she didn't want me to pay for her food. She was independent like that. I finished ordering fries, drinks, and desserts and paid.

Stella approached once I was done, and the girls had found us a booth, I followed them over with a tray of drinks and I went back for the food when Stella had finished ordering.

"What did you get?" I asked.

"Chicken sandwich." She smiled as we collected all of our food.

Once dinner was over, we rounded up the girls and made our way over to a grocery store and the girls raced each other to collect a cart.

I pulled out the list and began adding items to the cart while Stella went in her own direction to get some things she also needed. I was done with the dairy part of the list when the girls dumped a huge pile of snacks in the cart.

"Okay, but this isn't happening every time. We just need to stock up on snacks." I said firmly.

"Deal!" Cassie shook my hand.

"She seems like a handful." A man's voice said a few feet behind me.

I turned to see Mark pushing his cart down our aisle.

"Hey! What are you doing here?" I shook his hand.

"Favorite hang out." He joked.

"Those your girls?" He asked.

"Yeah, Cassie is the handful." I laughed.

Stella walked over with a basket and said hi to Mark.

"This is a bit of a reunion." Mark smiled.

"Yeah, what a chance meeting." Stella was uneasy. Nobody knew she was living on my front lawn.

Lilly walked over, pulled things out of Stella's basket, and asked what each item was.

"What's this?" Lilly pulled out a box with plan B written across it and 'emergency contraceptive' in white and pink.

Stella snatched it from her hands and began to walk away.

"Hey Stella, where are you going? You have to come home with us." I grabbed Lilly and covered her mouth to prevent her from talking anymore.

Mark was laughing loudly as he held himself up with a hand on my shoulder.

"Please don't say anything." I sighed. "It's not what it looks like." I added.

"Maybe we need to go and grab a beer for that conversation. Monday night football down at Crooked?" He asked.

"Sorry man, I got the girls full-time." I apologized.

"Go, I'll be there." Stella approached and rolled her eyes playfully.

"You don't have to." I whispered.

"No, I think it's a good idea you clear this up." She grinned.

"I agree with her. See you soon." Mark smiled at Stella and me. He made me feel like I was a mischievous child.

I walked around the store collecting the rest of the listed items while Cassie made her best attempts to throw in anything that caught her eye. Stella had finished her shopping and decided to wait outside, and I immediately felt a distance between us after the encounter with Mark.

Once we filled the cart with everything that would hopefully get us through a full week, I took the girls through the checkout where they snagged their final snacks.

"I think you guys can cook tomorrow." I squinted at them.

"Look at that bed shop over there." Cassie smiled.

"You did say we deserved them." Audrey fluttered her eyes at me, Lilly squeezed her hands together like she was praying, her eyes closed and her teeth showing with a big grin.

"Okay, go and pick a mattress. We'll pick up some frames somewhere else and upcycle them to match your rooms." I ordered but they had already run off testing all the mattresses.

"I want this one!" Lilly said as she sunk into a queen-sized plush bed with a pillow top.

"Not a bad price." I grabbed the tag to read the details.

"Do you have these in stock?" I asked the salesman approaching me.

"We do, I could have them delivered this week." He smiled.

"Audrey, Cassie. Try this one." I called them over.

"Oh, that's comfy!" Audrey approved.

"Stella, did you find one?" I asked and she strolled around the store.

"Huh?" She looked confused.

"Well, you're going to need a bed." I shrugged my shoulders. "Don't worry, I'm paying. It'll stay in the house; you just get to use it first." I added.

"That's generous, Dane." She smiled.

"Just furnishing the house. I think we're all a little sick of camping tables and chairs." I sighed.

"The only real furniture we have is a dining table, a couch, and some bar stools." Lilly shook her head as she tattled on me to the salesman whose eyes now lit up like a Christmas tree as he sniffed out some extra sales.

"Well, here's my card if you need anything else. I'll ring up an invoice for you." He shook my hand, and I was surprised he didn't try to sell me anything else.

"Just add a king size of the same mattress." I whispered as I watched over Stella.

"No worries." He smiled.

"Maybe a heated towel rack?" Audrey begged.

"Maybe, not." I laughed.

I went to the desk, paid for the mattresses, and organized delivery for the items towards the end of the week.

"Okay, let's go home." Cassie yawned.

We loaded the truck with the groceries and made our way home where Tux was sitting at the window anxiously waiting for some company.

Once we got inside and packed all the food away it was time for the girls to go to bed and Stella retreated to her van for an early night, she was exhausted from what seemed like an emotional day for her and Tux was happy back in his own space, it seemed at times he wasn't sure about living in such a big house.

I went to the girls' rooms and with the stencils Stella had brought I sprayed gold fairies and filigree all over Cassie and Lilly's rooms. In Audrey's room, I built shelves to the side of the window where Stella had suggested a reading nook, so I installed a bench seat and tucked storage cubes beneath it. I'd let Audrey choose her cushions and blankets for the space.

Most of their clothes were currently coming out of boxes and laundry baskets still aside from the one tallboy they'd been sharing. I scrolled through a local buy and sell and lined up a few items I could upcycle during the week.

Once I had all that planned, I went upstairs to the loft that Stella would soon occupy. It was an attic, but the open space made it a loft. The opening was small enough that I could just install a wide door to make it a room. The space had a high ceiling with dark beams. The walls needed another coat of paint, so I slicked on a layer of white that was leftover to help brighten it up a little and painted the window frames with a fresh coat of varnish.

It looked better already but the bathroom needed work. It had a free-standing bath that was in desperate need of a scrub and the feet needed a polish. The flooring was tiled in black and white checkers and gave the space a classic look and there was an old chandelier style light. It just needed some love with mold-free paint and a new showerhead and taps.

There was nowhere to hang towels, so I noted that down also and the heated shower rack sprang to mind.

It was Autumn now and already getting cold. I had heard winters in this region were awfully cold, often confining people to their homes for days. Pipes and toilets freezing over. The air was so cold it could freeze hot noodles in an instant. A far cry different to what I'd grown up with in Texas.

It was after midnight when I went to sleep on the couch. A storm blew outside, and the sound of the wind put me to sleep.

Stella

I woke up before my alarm from the deluge of rain and branches thrashing against my van. Tux was unsettled and paced back and forth through my one single walkway scratching at the door and desperately trying to wake me to get him out of there.

"TUX!" I grumbled and checked my phone for the time.

"5 am, you suck…" I yawned.

I got up out of bed and prayed that the front door was unlocked as I dragged myself across the lawn still half asleep trying to dodge and debris that was flying around. Tux was eager to get inside away from the cold wind and leaned against the door as I turned the handle opening the door to a warm, quiet home.

Dane was asleep on the couch with a single blanket over him. I went to check on the girls and to my surprise they were all covered up for once.

I took the chance to empty the clean washing into the dryer and throw on another load of washing before shutting the laundry door behind me as I sat in the kitchen cursing the kettle that whistled and craving an espresso shot but knowing Dane was only a stone's throw away from me, any fast movement might wake him.

I took myself to the other side of the couch where Tux was already curled up and I lay beside him and used him as a pillow. He huddled into my body to keep us both warm and I must have fallen asleep cause when I woke Cassie was hovering over us with Dane's phone taking photos of Tux and me.

"Good morning, Missy." I yawned.

"Good morning sleeping beauty." She smiled.

"Oh! What a lovely comment to wake up to." I pulled her down for a hug.

"Sorry, it wasn't my own organic work this time. Dad whispered it when he covered you with his blanket." She giggled.

"Well, that's very sweet. All girls love compliments, especially if their hair is looking like a bird's nest." I squeezed her.

"Oh! Hair…Can you braid my hair for today? Please?" She begged.

"Get the brush and hair ties." I nodded.

Cassie ran off to the bathroom to retrieve the hair stuff and Dane came down from the attic.

"Morning." He smiled as he didn't expect me to be awake.

"Good morning, sleeping beauty." I laughed.

"Fuck, nothing is a secret in this house." He rolled his eyes playfully.

"DOLLAR!" Audrey yelled from the doorway of Dane's room.

"Your words aren't safe. Best to say nothing." I grinned as I pulled myself up hoping Dane had made some coffee.

"GOT IT!" Cassie raced back into the room.

"Good work. I think I need some caffeine first, why don't you ask your sisters if they need their hair done too." I whispered.

"Okay." Cassie pointed to the steaming coffee pot.

"Pancakes or cereal?" Dane asked from the kitchen.

"Cereal." I yawned.

"Big night?" Dane teased.

"Ughh, the weather kept baby boy over there awake, therefore keeping me awake. Hence why we snuck in." I said as I pointed to Tux sleeping peacefully on the couch.

"I figured the weather might have played a role in that." He said.

"I'm still in your class today, right?" I asked.

"As far as I know." he replied.

"Good, you'll find me asleep in the timeout corner." I laughed as I sipped at a mug of hot black coffee.

"Hmmm, no. I think I'll make you take the class for morning fitness while I write out the first lesson." He smiled.

"Why do I feel like you aren't joking?" I froze.

"Cause I'm not." Dane was stern and the SEAL in him began to show.

"Fine, but star jumps and stretches are the height of my ability." I groaned.

"Two laps of the obstacle course on top of that…" Dane said.

"Are you being serious?" I glared at him.

"I'm not doing it to be mean. It'll help wake you up. Some nice fresh air." He grumbled.

"Guess I'll wear sneakers then." I growled as I walked to find the girls in the bathroom.

"Dads on a warpath, beware." Audrey whispered as she closed the door with all four of us girls inside.

"I just caught that." I whispered back.

"What's up his ass?" Cassie scowled.

"A big fat poo!" Lilly giggled.

"Mom text him." Audrey sighed.

"Oh dear… should we be worried?" I asked.

"He didn't say anything, he just threw the phone and now he's moody." Audrey said expressively.

"Keep your heads low till we get to school, girls. If you need anything maybe come find me instead." I said as I braided Cassie's hair.

"Got it!" Lilly smiled as she brushed through her long hair.

"Can I have two braids? I'd like curly waves when I wake up tomorrow." Audrey asked.

"I think that will look amazing on you!" I nodded.

"BREAKFAST!" Dane banged on the door and scared Cassie.

"Lil if you and Cass are done why don't you go together." I smiled.

"Okay." Lilly hugged me tight.

The two younger girls went to eat their cereal and Audrey turned to me, her eyes a little wet but I could tell she was fighting back tears.

"Are you okay?" I hugged her.

"I just wish she'd leave us alone. Every time Dad seems happy, she has to ruin it." She cried.

"Oh Audrey, it's hard for them. They probably have a lot of issues to work through." I sighed.

"We have a little brother, he's only a few months old and we've never met him." Audrey dried her eyes.

"Maybe that's triggered her to reach out. She misses you guys." I said trying to comfort her.

"I'm done with her. All she'll do is let us down." Audrey parted her hair, and I began to braid while she wiped her face with a warm flannel.

"I'm here if you ever want to talk about it. I'll just listen." I said as I tied off her last braid and walked for the door.

"Stella…" Audrey stopped me.

"Thank you for being here. It's nice to talk to someone about this who isn't dad. He shelters me from it, but I'm not blind to what goes on. Cassie and Lilly are too young to even notice. You know we don't even know who the father of our brother is." She grumbled angrily.

"Have you ever thought about calling your mom and asking?" I questioned.

"I don't want to give her the satisfaction." Audrey seemed so mature, and so terrifying that she had such a coldness to her.

The Audrey I knew was quiet but sweet and so family-orientated. But I guess this woman had hurt and broken her family. She was right to be angry.

"Come on…" Dane knocked at the door.

I opened the door and Dane stood there, his hair a little wild, beard untrimmed, and dark demeanor about him.

Today I'd stay out of his way and do my job.

Dane

I was being a complete ass, to everyone. But I couldn't stop. Being woken up to a text from Gina was the only thing that could ruin my day.

Who's that woman in the girls new YouTube video?

A nanny

Awfully young to be a nanny. How are the girls?

You have no right to ask about them. Text me again and I'll block your number.

She didn't reply after that. And I was glad, but not proud of the way I'd handled things this morning.

The short drive to school was awkwardly quiet and the day in the class with Stella was worse. She was short with me, gave me one-word replies only, and mostly nodded.

But she did take the class for fitness and made them run more laps than I had suggested, and it seemed I had put her in an equally bad mood. Stella sat in the cafeteria for lunch and Cassie, Heather, and Lilly joined her. Audrey often opted for the library and was usually allowed as long as she only had cold food.

Cassie glared at me in only a way Cassie could. She had daggers for me. Lilly made eye contact only to cross her arms and *hmph* at me.

Little did they all know our happiness in this little town was under threat. Gina could tip my life upside down with one phone call to a lawyer demanding shared custody.

Or Stella could leave, and it wouldn't just be me who would feel crushed. The girls had adopted her now and she felt like family. I knew had to keep my dick in my pants instead of chasing her with it.

"Stella?" I rested my hand on her shoulder.

"Yes, Dane." She growled.

"Okay, I deserve that." She stood up and moved over by the window with me away from any students.

"What is your problem? Is it me? Cause if it's what happened between us, I'll leave. The girls don't deserve your moods." She hissed.

"Gina… She saw the girl's new video and scalded me about you." I sighed.

"Fuck…" she said under her breath.

"If I know Gina she won't stop there, but she's quiet for now." I answered. "Don't tell the girls please." I begged.

"They know. I don't know how but they filled me in when I did their hair." I confessed.

"Audrey. She doesn't miss a beat." I huffed.

"Let's get through the day. I'll take the girls home and cook with them. I think that beer with Mark came just in time." She gave me sweet puppy eyes like she felt sorry for me and went to brush my arm but realized where we were.

"What would I do without you?" I smiled for the first time today.

"You'll figure it out. But for now, I'm here." She smiled back at me softly.

"Yeah, good idea." I walked away a little hurt.

Stella was being so clear about how emotionally unavailable she was, and I wanted to respect that, but she filled my home with fun, good food, hair braiding, and warm hugs, she had put me back together, and for a time I forgot about the ugly divorce that was playing out in the background.

It had only been a few weeks, but we felt like a family again.

Back in class Stella was keeping a low profile and had some of the kids help her restock the hygiene and snack drawers we had taken over from the previous teacher. Duluth had a mix of wealthy and poor families so accommodating basic needs felt like a no-brainer to ensure everyone always felt comfortable, clean, and fed.

The day was finally over, and back home Stella was juggling the girls into showers, simultaneously cooking and folding laundry while I quickly collected furniture pieces before I went to the bar.

"Are you sure it's okay if I go?" I leaned over the bench while she breaded chicken breast.

"YES! Please go." Cassie yelled from the couch.

"Okay, I know when I'm not wanted." I frowned.

"We love you daddy." Lilly jumped up for a hug.

"I love you too Lil." I hugged her back.

"Go and have some fun." Stella ordered.

I went out to the front where my taxi waited for me, hopped in, and gave directions to the bar Mark had suggested.

When I arrived, Mark was in the car park waiting for me and we went in together and ordered our first round of beers and wings.

"Thanks, bro. I needed this." I said as I took a swig of my beer.

"Sounds like you've had a rough trot. Raising those girls alone can't be easy?" He wondered.

"It's been the hardest job I've ever had. It's odd. I've known them all their lives and raised them and changed diapers and fed them, but somehow, I feel like I'm only learning now who they really are. I had no idea Audrey read two books a week. I had no idea Cassie liked the color teal. Lilly, I didn't know how much she loved me." I sighed.

"Of course she loves you!" Mark smacked my shoulder.

"No, like really. She's always reassuring me and reminding me mistakes are okay. She's so kind." I smiled.

"And Stella?" Mark prodded.

"Stella is perfect." I grinned.

"You gotta give me more than that." Mark grunted.

"We did hook up…" I confessed as I tried not to elaborate on the finer details. "But it won't happen again." I added and skulled back the second half of my beer.

"Come on, she's pretty hot. Clearly, she's into you." Mark pressed.

"I have no doubt the feelings are mutual, but I think she cares more about the girls. She doesn't want to start something just to up and leave. She's a gypsy and maybe one day she'll settle, but it isn't now." I started dipping a buffalo wing into some blue cheese sauce.

"What's her deal?" Mark asked.

"Her best friend and her were meant to travel together and basically do what she's doing now. She was killed by a drunk driver a few years ago before they got started. She kinda shuts off after that." I explained.

"Her parents are coming to stay soon. Maybe they'll give me a bit more insight." I pondered.

"That's rough. No wonder she's a bit numb." Mark added.

"Shitty thing to happen to both of them." I agreed.

"But you guys did bang? I can tell!" Mark tried to liven up the mood.

I laughed at his enthusiasm. "Yes, and it was better with her than anyone else." I said with regret. Saying it out loud gave it so much weight and validation.

"Well, if you guys decide to date, I'll babysit." Mark gave me a high five.

"Thanks." I laughed.

Our burgers arrived with a loaded plate of fries and another round of beer with two shots of whiskey.

"Are you trying to get me drunk?" I laughed.

"Bottoms up." Mark raised his shot glass to mine, and we sunk them quickly.

Three more beers later we shared a cab all the way home along with half our life stories. By now Mark knew all about Gina and I learned he had a newborn baby with a one-night stand he was now trying to date but was finding it hard not to rush things when the baby came first. He had good intentions and the mother seemed like she was in for the long run, but they weren't living together yet, even though he wanted to so he could be with his son more.

"Thanks for a good night!" I fist-pumped him as I climbed out of the cab.

"See you tomorrow." The cab drove away.

A white car was parked out the front of my house in the street that I didn't recognize. I could hear screaming coming from inside and I expected the girls to be having a dance party and I was excited to see them after the rough day I'd had.

"DAD!" Audrey ran out of the house and hugged me crying.

"Don't let her take us." She wept.

"What the fuck?" I raced into the house and Gina was there trying to yell at Cassie. Stella was blocking Gina from her, and Audrey whispered that Lilly was hiding and had locked herself in the bathroom.

"What do you think you're doing in my house?" I yelled.

Gina turned to face me and from the back door, a face I recognized poured through.

"James? Why are you here?" I questioned.

"Oh, nobody told you?" James asked.

James was my younger cousin who lived around the corner from us.

"It was you? Helping yourself to my wife?" I approached him pushed him back outside and closed the screen door behind us.

"It wasn't like that. It just happened." James put his arms up and surrendered, trying to evade a fight.

I had no words. I fisted my hands behind the back of my head and looked around. First, at the man who stood before me, who was once a kid I taught to fish and string a line. Inside Stella was consoling Cassie. I could hear Audrey trying to get into the bathroom with

Lilly and then there was a stroller with a baby boy in it. Tux was behind me and knew something was up and he snarled wildly at James.

"You son of a bitch. Why couldn't you two just leave us in peace? You can have her!" I growled.

I didn't mean to hit him, but I was so angry from hearing the girls screaming I just snapped. I pummeled my fist into his cheek and Tux barked as he threatened to hit me back, but I had him in a choke hold on the ground before he could get back up or land any hits.

"Tux!" Stella called. He raced to her, tearing through the screen door with no effort at all and he followed beside her and Cassie while she went to find Audrey and Lilly.

"Girls! Come with me." She banged on the bathroom door and Gina went to check on her baby.

I could see Stella locking Tux in with the girls in my bedroom and she came out alone and faced off with Gina.

"GET OUT! Neither of you are welcome here. Audrey has my phone. She is calling the police." Stella became stern but Gina refused.

"I'm not leaving my girls with that wild beast in there with them." She hissed.

"Tux saved Cassie and Audrey. Maybe you should thank him. He is more of a parent than you are." Stella snarled.

James stopped fighting back and we both sat up as we watched a war of words unfold.

"I can't believe you did this to me?" I said with disappointment, all I could do was shake my head at him and a shadow of regret washed over his face as he looked at me with sadness.

"She said you knew…I wouldn't have come here last minute if I didn't think you knew. Dane, I'm a lot of things, a shitty cousin, but wouldn't spring this on you." He sighed.

"Well, she lied. And you're a piece of shit for falling for her crap and having a baby with her. Now we're even more related than we used to be." I pulled myself up and went inside.

"LEAVE." I stood over Gina and made myself known.

"See you in court." She smiled.

"We don't want to live with you!" Lilly appeared from the room.

"Lilly? I thought we were best friends?" Gina froze and tried to soften her tone.

"And then you left us without even saying goodbye." Lilly cried and ran to Stella. I knew that would cut Gina deep.

"I was confused. I'm sorry. You can come home with me and Uncle James and your baby brother." She pleaded.

"No, we aren't leaving Dad. We aren't like you." Audrey came and stood in front of me like a shield, and I felt a tear stray down my cheek as the girls all came together and held hands creating a wall.

"I have three flights booked for tomorrow for you to all come home with us." She cried.

"Well, you better get a store credit." Cassie poked her tongue at her.

"You're really going to leave me without my girls?" Gina begged.

"Don't gaslight them, they've been very clear. There's the door." I growled.

James pushed the stroller out first and Gina turned to look at us all once more with a longing in her eyes I might have once felt sorry for.

"Keep walking!" Cassie snarled.

The girls were worked up and now that I finally had time to look around it was clear she had been here long enough to make a mess. There was tomato sauce splashed over the walls, uncooked chicken schnitzels on the floors and the oven door had been broken and a trail of blood led to Stella.

I grabbed her hand and found a gash across her hand.

"I'll support you if you press charges." I reached for a tea towel to compress the wound.

"No, it's superficial. She's, their mom. I can't do that." She shook her head.

"She clearly came at you and attacked you." I pressed.

"I think she was just worked up about not knowing who I was, living with her kids. I get it." Stella held the towel over her hand.

She was a better person than I was. I could never be that chill after what just unfolded, and I'd be sending her the bill for the oven.

"Let me take some photos just to be safe?" I asked to which she nodded and agreed.

I pulled out my phone and snapped some photos of everything that was now out of place.

"I think you need stitches." I pulled the tea towel away to look at her hand.

"Maybe, I'll head down to urgent care and see what they say." She grabbed her keys.

"I'll drive you!" I grabbed the keys from her.

"You've had a lot to drink." She argued. "Look it's really not that deep, I'll cover it and see how it is in the morning. It's getting late and we all need to get to bed. Work and school tomorrow." She yawned.

"Okay." I agreed.

I went into my room to check on the girls who had taken themselves to bed after all the confusion and they were all cuddled up together in my bed with blankets on.

Stella

I woke up extra early today and took myself to a pharmacist to get patched up properly. I was right, I didn't need stitches, but it was right where I flexed my hand, and keeping it dry was going to be difficult. The pharmacist gave me a note to take the rest of the week off work and I gratefully accepted.

When I got home there was hot coffee dripping, but the girls were still asleep. Dane was cooking pancakes and looking through an iPad for an oven repairer.

"Hey, you headed out early?" Dane said.

"Yeah, I just got my hand checked." I replied.

"Stitches?" He asked.

"No, luckily. But I got a week off work." I smiled.

"I'm really sorry I wasn't here when this all went down." He sighed and I noticed he had made a good effort to clean up the mess and he even patched the oven door with some cardboard, so it didn't cut anyone else.

"You didn't know that was going to happen." I said, trying to assure him I was okay.

"Thank you for keeping my girls safe." He smiled.

I didn't mean to, but I leaned in onto his chest and I just hugged him. He immediately wrapped his arms around me, and he held me in his warmth and the buttery scent of pancakes made this all the more enjoyable.

He rubbed my back and kissed my forehead and I tucked myself into him tighter, never wanting this feeling of security to end.

I wrapped my arms around his neck, and he lifted me up onto the bench before I could protest, we were kissing as our hands explored each other's bodies and my one good hand was in his pants stroking his length and he had a hand up my dress inside me.

"FUCK." I bit my lip trying to stay quiet.

"Shhh." He kissed me hoping it would keep me quiet but with every plunge he made me wetter and then he added another finger.

"Dane!" I arched my back.

He slid his fingers out of me, and I tightened my arms around his neck as he carried me to the bathroom and undressed me.

"We shouldn't..." but Dane pressed his fingers to my lips and silenced me.

He pushed down his briefs and his cock sprung up. He unbuttoned the front of my dress and pushed it off my shoulders and he was excited to remove my thong and slide his fingers through my gooey juices that craved him.

I led him into the shower and ran the water into a corner to hopefully cover any sound we might make. He picked me up and slid his girth inside me slowly so I could be reaccustomed to his size. I grasped his shoulders as he held my weight through my thighs, and I greedily bounced up and down on him hungry for more. I couldn't be close enough and he registered my cues as he plunged into me as deep as possible by letting my body weight fall a little harder each time.

He gripped my ass, playing with handfuls of me squeezing gently and then sucking at my breasts. He leaned me against the cold tiles that made me arch further onto him while I held onto the windowsill and curtain rail as he pounded me hard and fast. I couldn't hold on any longer and my body convulsed and thrashed as I came for him, my tight slit clenching as he drained every drop of cum into me and I grazed my clit over him still aching for more. He dropped to his knees, licked at my warm and sensitive bud, and gently circled his tongue around me as I fell onto his hot mouth. He raked his tongue back and forth so softly the explosion came by surprise, and I accidentally squealed a little too loud as he fingered me enjoying the wooshes of my muscles flexing around him.

"That was amazing." I dropped to his level, climbed on top of him, and kissed him passionately.

"What are you doing to me?" He brushed my hair off my face.

"Making you burn pancakes by the smell of it." I giggled.

"FUCK!" He exclaimed.

He gently moved me off him jumped up and wrapped a towel around his waist and ran off to the kitchen.

I knew I couldn't follow in the same way, so I tried to stand up and wash myself without falling over.

It was proving difficult, and I was feeling pretty grateful to have a week off work. I'd need a day just to recover from the sex and didn't feel guilty one bit.

I rinsed off then wrapped myself in a towel once I was done dried off and put my dress back on, so I didn't look suspicious if the girls were up.

Dane was in the kitchen, now fully dressed flipping a new batch of pancakes and grinning at me from ear to ear. I walked over and sat at the bench where he had just filled me with his fingers, and he fed me a pancake, syrup, and butter dripping down my chin and he licked it off down my neck and back up to kiss me.

"You are so going to get us caught." I said as I kissed him back and took the rest of the pancake.

"Do we have to hide?" He sighed.

"Let's just not label this." I suggested.

"Okay, I'll do it your way. But don't go breaking my heart, Gypsy." He kissed me again and I liked the sound of that new nickname.

"Dane…" I growled.

"I'm just kidding." But I could tell he wasn't, and I knew suddenly he felt more than what I was capable of giving back to him.

"I'll get the girls up." I jumped down and wiped myself off with a paper towel.

"Thanks." His voice followed me as I opened the door to his room.

The girls were all piled on top of each other sleeping in weird positions that looked like they'd give me back aches and endless visits to a chiropractor.

"Girls." I said as I dimmed the lights and tried to pull them off of each other.

"Ughh, no!" Cassie grumbled.

"Sorry, but yes. Dad made pancakes." Audrey's nose pricked up and she sniffed around.

"Smells like someone burnt them." Lilly twitched her nose unpleasantly.

"Some, but there's good ones coming out now. You know the first ones down are always drafts!" I tried to make a believable excuse.

"That is true…" Cassie took a long-exaggerated sniff of the air as she slowly pulled her legs over the side of the bed.

"Just five more minutes." Audrey yanked the blanket over her head.

"Fine, but I'm sending Cassie in to wake you if you aren't up." I teased.

"You monster!" She popped her eyes out of the covers and squinted at me.

"Stella, you're falling from grace." Lilly whispered.

"I've got a week off work and a lot of drawers to sand, a mattress delivery and I'm pretty sure three bedrooms to decorate…or you could be late for school and hold that all up." I joked.

"OKAY! I'm up." Audrey sprung to her feet.

"Knew that would get you." I winked.

"I kinda like sleeping in here with you guys." Lilly said as she skipped behind the two older girls out to the kitchen.

"I do not share the same feelings." Audrey messed her hair.

"Oh, is it because I farted?" Lilly asked.

"Woah, good morning girls. Can we leave all the farts and fart talk back there! I have something for you." Dane spun around and grabbed a tray covered with a tea towel.

He ordered the girls to close their eyes with his army hand signals and they all smiled wide and shut their eyes as he uncovered a platter of pancakes covered in Nutella, strawberries, a dusting of powdered sugar, and some blueberries for a little extra razzle-dazzle.

"Okay, you can open them." He smiled proudly as he placed the tray down and uncovered his work.

"OH, MY GOODNESS!" Lilly screamed.

"You outdid yourself, old man." Cassie said as she took a pancake and folded it like a taco and took her first bite.

"I'm impressed." Audrey got up and hugged him and he held her tight and kissed her forehead.

"Thank you for sticking up for me yesterday girls." Dane got serious and they all took a seat and started eating.

"We hate her..." Audrey sighed as she chomped into another pancake.

"She speaks for all of us." Cassie nodded.

"Agreed." Lilly smiled with Nutella all over her face.

"Girls, she's still your mom. Whatever happened between us shouldn't become your issue." Dane explained.

"That's not it. She didn't just leave you, she left *us*. Without so much as a goodbye. We didn't know where she was going or who with." Audrey grumbled.

"Come to think of it, Uncle James was around a lot." Cassie stroked her chin as she thought back.

"He was nice though." Lilly intervened.

"Girls the point is she has a right to see you. It's my job to make sure you get the best upbringing and if you miss out on a mother for the rest of your childhood, you'll be in therapy the rest of your lives." Dane sighed.

"Stella does more than mom ever did! Audrey washed my school shoes in the sink one time because I stepped in cat poo, and mom was too grossed out to touch them." Cassie scowled.

"Oh?" Dane's eyes widened.

"And that time you got COVID! She opened the door, shoved food in with a baseball bat, and made us all hide when you needed the bathroom. You had to ring a bell to let us know you were coming out of your room!" Cassie was exploding with detail after detail, and I backed away to Audrey's room to give them some privacy.

"I'm never going back there!" Cassie screamed.

"Okay, I'm not going to make you. But if this goes to court, you need to tell them everything you've told me." Dane went around the bench and hugged Cassie as I closed the door behind me.

Audrey's room looked beautiful. Dane had installed a bench seat beside the window and a black curtain rod. The bench was bare but nothing, a few layers of foam, a staple gun, and some velvet couldn't fix. Under the bench were storage boxes and a piece of paper with delivery dates for two bookcases and a mini black chandelier.

Dane was planning to surprise her with something she'd only dreamed of, and I couldn't wait to see it pieced together.

I went to the garage to search for a staple gun once I heard the girls running around getting dressed and Dane clanging dishes in the sink.

Dane poked his head into the garage, "Stella, there's a bunch of furniture being delivered today. Can you take it? Most are secondhand and need some love. You'll know the difference." He smiled.

"Sure! Do you have a staple gun by any chance?" I questioned.

"In one of the boxes that says shed." He laughed.

"There's like eight of those…" I sighed.

"Pretty sure it's in the one that says SHEB instead of SHED." He laughed.

I laughed also and turned back and walked to the shed to look once more and this time found the staple gun.

"Success!" I strolled past the kitchen with my victory and out to my van where I knew I had black velvet I had once tried to use as a curtain because it was on sale in a dollar bin at Michaels. But it was too heavy and made the wire droop so was then added to the draw of mayhem.

I fished through the deep draw and found it below a few other pieces of experimental fabric and hauled it all inside.

"Hey! What is that?" Cassie tried to chase me.

"No, stay back." I shoved it all down my shirt, but Audrey tackled me from the height of the couch and Tux became excited and brought over his ball.

"Get her!" Lilly piled on top of us as giggling echoed through the mostly empty home and Dane tried to peel them off me.

"RUN!" He shouted as he got Audrey off of me.

I sprinted for the room and locked the door behind me.

The girls sighed loudly as I leaned against the door trying to catch my breath and I heard Dane telling them one room could be finished as soon as today. They all rejoiced in the thought, and I went back to work.

In one corner was a pile of old throwaways we had planned to use as rags and amongst it was a thick memory foam pillow that had begun to sink too much in the middle. There was some glue in the box of random bits and pieces where the paint had taken up residence and a Stanley knife too. I cut the foam through the middle to create two thick cushions and sized them against the bench. They were just the right size lengthways, and I glued them down with what I knew was probably the wrong glue.

Once I heard everyone leaving, I ran out to find a plate of pancakes tucked away in the fridge with '*Gypsy*' written on the saran wrap with a sharpie. Butterflies filled my stomach and pulled them out and sat at the bench eating them as I wrote a list of everything I wanted to achieve today. I wanted to finish Audrey's room.

The doorbell rang just as I finished my breakfast, and a large white truck was being unloaded by a few men.

"Where would you like these?" One man asked.

"Oh woah. Okay, can I sort them in the rooms quickly?" The man nodded.

"These three follow me." It was two bookcases and a new set of drawers. They were for Audrey.

Next was a wooden bedframe with tall posts and a set of drawers, both needing some TLC but excellent pieces.

Lastly was a dressing table, a matching stool, a wide dresser, and a white bedframe with plenty of potential.

"Thank you." I waved the men off and I got to work installing the bookshelves to be inward-facing around the large window.

Everything fit snuggly once I had stapled the black velvet onto the bench. Any extra fabric I stapled to the base of the bench so it would act as a curtain and cover the storage cubes.

Once I vacuumed the floors in each room, I took a cab to Michaels. I was feeling a little too lazy to unhook my van and it wasn't that far away.

I found a fluffy grey rug that would suit Audrey's room perfectly, some new bed sheets, some comfy cushions for the reading nook, and two throw blankets I knew she'd love.

I then tackled the list for Cassie and Lilly, each getting similar things to match their rooms.

Once home I designated the shopping to the right rooms and called the mattress store to let them know I was home and ready for them.

I spoke with a kind man who understood that I was on a time limit and offered me express delivery within the next hour and I accepted.

"They'll be there once they've loaded all the mattresses." The man said.

It was almost the middle of the day, and I snapped photos and texted them to Dane.

> Audrey should have a bedroom tonight, washing the bedding now and the mattresses should be here soon, he even threw in some mattress protectors 

> I thought they were arriving later in the week?

> I can be persuasive...

> I know! Good job.

The bedding finished in the washer, and I went to transfer them to the dryer and pulled out the last load of clothes that I'd placed in there the day before yesterday. I needed to get better at keeping up with the washing for five people.

I sat on the floor with the door open and began sorting clothes into baskets for each person. Socks were the worst, underwear came second. Lilly's were tiny so that was easy, but Cassie and Audrey were only one size apart.

The front door opened, and I heard the noise Dane's keys make when they rattle.

"In here." I yelled from the laundry as he followed my voice and he leaned against the door frame and smiled down at me.

"Hi…" He smiled back. "Shouldn't you be teaching a class?" I asked.

"Mark's covering for me…there's something in that delivery you can't see yet." He whispered a little embarrassed.

"Is it a sex swing?" I teased.

"Do you want a sex swing?" His eyes widened.

"No, I'm a little achy just from the shower." I laughed.

A knock at the door interrupted us and Dane sprang off the doorframe and off down the hallway to answer the door.

"Don't come out!" He yelled and I knew he meant me.

I could hear him just slightly directing two men into different rooms.

They were done in ten minutes and Dane raced back down the hall.

"I gotta get back." He said as I stood up.

"Okay see you tonight." I smiled.

He turned back quickly, bent down to kiss me, closed his eyes so he wouldn't see my reaction, and ran out the front door.

If he kept doing things like that it might make me want to stay but I wasn't ready for that.

I distracted myself by removing the plastic sleeves from the beds and covering them with mattress protectors and finally all their clean fresh new linen.

I'd be able to let Audrey in tonight. All she needed to do was arrange her books, and clothes and get Dane to hang her festoon lights.

I had about an hour to go before the others got home and with my good hand, I roughly sanded the furniture in Cassie's room and kicked myself for vacuuming too soon.

It didn't need a lot of work, just the top layer smoothed and a new layer of varnish on all the furniture to make it all match. It would have to be dark, but it went with the theme she had asked for.

I wiped down the furniture with a damp cloth once I was done, let it air off, and then began to apply the lacquer in smooth long strokes.

Cassie's room wouldn't be done tonight and with the smell of the varnish, I'd need to crack a window overnight.

I finished just in time for the front door to open and the girls raced in, Tux rejoiced to have company since I kept locking him away from the fumes in the bedrooms.

"Go shower!" Dane ordered.

"How'd you go?" he asked.

"Audrey's is done." I smiled.

He opened the door and beamed happiness. "You should show her." Dane rubbed my shoulder, and I held his hand.

Audrey knocked on the door and I invited her in. Her eyes squinted as she tried not to look.

"Open your eyes!" I pulled her hands down.

"NO WAY!" She shouted at the empty bookcases and reading bench.

She moved around the room slowly, now dropping to the floor to pat the rug, examining the empty drawers, and clapping with excitement at how big they were, she hugged the box of mini festoon lights I had left for her on her bed and the small black birdcage style chandelier so she could choose where to hand it.

"I don't even know what to say." Her eyes welled up with happiness.

"You're welcome." I smiled.

She fell into me and hugged me. "Your dad helped too." I laughed.

"Thanks, Dad." She moved to hug him next.

"Well, you better start filling those drawers." Dane brushed her hair off her face.

"Screw the clothes. The books!" She beamed.

"I guess that's my cue to go and haul in all those boxes." Dane's jaw dropped.

"Right on!" She smiled.

I left the room to lay on the couch with Tux for a moment to let her enjoy her new space and I was thrilled to see how much she loved it.

"Me next? We're going from eldest to youngest?" Cassie plopped herself down next to me.

"Not intentionally, but that seems to be how it's coming along." I answered.

Good, Lilly won't mind waiting another day." Cassie smiled.

"A day?" I asked.

"Mine should be done tomorrow, right?" she questioned.

"If all the fumes are gone then yes." I nodded. "But I can't promise I'll have all the curtains up, I'm a little short." I laughed.

"DADDDYY!" Cassie yelled and Dane stumbled past with a box of books.

"Yes, boss?" Dane huffed.

"You need to hang the curtains around my bed, Stella is too small." She ordered.

"Yes ma'am!" He laughed.

"Tonight…" She grinned.

"And just who do you think is cooking or ordering dinner if we are doing all that?" Dane asked.

"Give me your phone, we are more than capable of ordering dinner." She placed her hand out for his phone.

He tried to resist but her smile soon turned sour, and he reluctantly agreed.

"You guys will send me broke." He laughed.

"SEALs get good bonuses." She sassily flicked her hand at him.

"Who said?" Dane questioned.

"We googled it." She replied.

He shook his head and raised his eyebrows. "You know I don't do that anymore." He rebuffed.

"I thought you were going back?" Her face was saddened.

"Things change. You're stuck with me." He kissed her forehead and grabbed the box of books as Audrey called out for him.

"Don't worry Cass, he won't go back, he loves being with you girls." I sat up and hugged her.

"When can we make our costumes?" She changed the subject immediately.

"Well, we can start this week if we get the rooms done soon." I smiled. "When is it?" I asked.

"Two weeks." She answered.

"You know, I think my parents will be here then! They'll love you guys." I smiled.

"Are they staying with us?" She asked.

"I told them to get a hotel." I replied.

"And I told them they can stay here!" Dane shouted from the room.

"He outranks you..." She laughed.

"He does, but he'll regret it." I laughed too.

Cassie began to browse UberEATS for dinner options and I shut my eyes while Tux nestled in beside me.

Dane

I was amazed by how fast the rooms were coming along. Stella worked at such a fast speed and even the other two rooms were close to done. Once I unloaded all of Audrey's books I went to Cassie's room and started hanging the curtains from each beam of her bedframe to the next.

It looked almost identical to Fiona's bed from Shrek when she was locked in the castle. The teal walls made it look even more majestic and the gold stencils set the room off to make it look woodsy and magical. Stella did a good job staining everything with a dark wood varnish.

I moved everything into position and began draping the fake vines from the curtain rod from over the window, tacked it to the roof and then over to the bed, then more over the upcycled full-length mirror.

"I'm happy with that." I said to myself as I left the room and shut the door behind me.

"She's in the shower." Stella said almost half asleep on the couch and slumped her arm in the direction of the bathroom. My Phone was on the cushion beside her with the tracker open and an order from Taco Bell on the way.

Lilly was sitting beside Tux with her headphones on and iPad in hand watching some random YouTube family shopping in Target.

Since nobody seemed to need me, I went to Lilly's room. There were fairies spray painted in gold and white on her lilac walls from a sheet of stencils. Her bedframe needed to be retouched and I opened the window and laid down some old bed sheets and began spray painting them.

The wind was doing a good job of sucking out the fumes from all the sprays and lacquers. I heard a car coming up the driveway through the open window.

The driver honked their horn and I walked to the front door to accept the food.

"Girls!" I called as I placed the bags of food down on the table.

One by one they all sat down at the table. Stella was now asleep on the couch.

"Should we wake her?" Cassie whispered.

"She's had a big day. Let her sleep." I smiled at the girls. "You are going to love your rooms; she's done a great job." I said proudly.

"Can we please see the others, just a peek!" Audrey begged.

"Well, Stella should get to see your reactions." I winked.

"Speaking of bedrooms, can I get your help to do up the loft for Stella?" I whispered over the table.

"She's staying?" Lilly's eyes bulged excitedly.

"Probably through fall and winter, but she's welcome always." I smiled.

"When are you going to ask her out?" Cassie said as she bit into a taco.

"I was thinking about that too. Would it be okay if I asked her to the school dance?" I peered at them waiting for a response.

"YES!" Audrey cheered.

"Finally…" Cassie scoffed.

"Let's not get ahead of ourselves. She might say no." I sighed.

"Well, it's hardly a date. You need to go somewhere private and romantic, not your kids Halloween dance." Audrey crossed her arms.

"I just don't have the time or sitters to go on a proper date." I sighed.

I knew it and so did they. Time was hard, it was the whole reason Stella ended up living here, I was low on time to do things around the house and spend time with the girls.

With her here things were getting done and we could even tick off bedroom modifications now. The piles of laundry were getting done and instead of buying new towels every week, I had clean fresh towels in the cupboard. Our beds had sheets on them, food was being cooked. And my balls weren't so blue.

I couldn't afford to fuck this up and scare her off.

"She's snoring." Lilly snickered.

"Maybe we should put her to bed?" Audrey asked me.

"Yeah, come open the doors for me to the van." I said to Audrey as I walked over to the couch.

I scooped my arms underneath Stella and carried her through the front door as Audrey raced ahead to the van and opened the door and I stepped up into the van. Audrey pulled back the blankets and moved out of the small walkway and I placed her down gently and removed her shoes.

I pulled the blanket over her, and she rolled over and nuzzled into the fluffy pillows.

"Daddy, who's that?" Audrey whispered.

"That was Stella's best friend, Ana." I sighed.

"Was?" She asked.

"She's not here anymore." I replied.

"Where did she go?" Cassie asked as she poked her head in.

"Come inside girls, I'll explain." I closed the van door and shut off the lights.

I walked back into the house with the girls and sat down at the table. Lilly was on the couch with Tux watching a Disney movie.

"Ana was killed in an accident." I whispered softly.

"Oh!" Cassie was speechless.

"I bet she misses her a lot." Audrey sighed and I saw tears build in her eyes.

"It's been hard for Stella. She's got us though and Tux. We'll look after her as long as she wants us to." I smiled.

"What about when she leaves and she's alone again?" Audrey asked.

"Maybe she'll decide she doesn't want to be alone anymore." Cassie said with her spark of optimism.

"I guess that's up to her to decide." I added.

"Don't be so glum!" Audrey growled at me.

"Yeah! Don't chase her away." Cassie grumbled at me.

"Okay, I had a rough day and now you know why. We're my feelings not valid?" I asked.

"Yes, but you can't take it out on us." Cassie became serious.

"I know, I am very sorry. I'm quite surprised your mom hasn't shown up again." I confessed.

"I think she was shocked when *we* stood up to her." Audrey added.

"She was hurt." I sighed.

"She started this, you just picked up the pieces. You have nothing to feel bad for." Cassie said.

"I uprooted you from your home and moved you as far north to the cheapest house I could get." I slumped back into my chair.

"We like it here! We love our new house, and our school is pretty good too." Lilly shouted.

"Hey, big ears! Feel like helping me paint some walls?" I asked the girls as I looked at my watch.

"Definitely yes!" Cassie jumped up from her chair and immediately bolted up the stairs.

I explained the idea to them, and they instantly liked the idea of a room divider and the double bench that Stella had suggested. Audrey was mapping out an area for a bookcase and Cassie was taping down newspaper in the bathroom. Lilly was already painting, and I was on the ladder painting the top sections.

Audrey went into the bathroom to help Cassie with polishing the hardware that was going to stay and I removed the pieces that were too old.

"Okay, this is mold-free paint. Do you think you can paint this whole room?" I smiled.

"Give me that!" Cassie smirked as she snatched the paintbrush and Audrey hauled the pot of paint into the bathroom after laying down an old sheet on top of the newspaper.

I let the girls go for it with the paint and they kept a window open for ventilation. They painted the door white too and wrote a list of things to buy at Lowes.

-Gold taps

-Gold towel rack (heated)

-New curtain

They had a vision for the space, and I was quite grateful it wasn't fluro or some wild eccentric color. Surprisingly was a lot like my own.

We'd been at this for a few hours, and we had finally finished all the walls. The bathroom was done except for the things the girls listed and now all we needed were bed sheets and a valance since the bed was an ensemble.

The space in front of the window was reserved for office space and bookshelves and I sat on the ground with Cassie's iPad as we browsed furniture websites for bookcases and benches when we heard the front door creak and footsteps.

"Shhh…" I said as I heard Stella rustling in the fridge for leftover tacos.

"That one!" Lilly squealed when she saw a bookcase with a ladder. "I can pretend I'm Belle!" She leaped up and swooped across the room dancing.

"Consider our position disclosed." Audrey laughed.

"Hello?" Stella called softly as she climbed the stairs.

"WOAH! This looks cool, I thought you guys were all asleep. It's 2 am." She yawned through a mouthful of food.

" Is it really?" I checked my watch.

"I'm so not going to school, Dad!" Cassie fell onto the bed and yawned.

"What she said." Lilly did the same and Audrey tugged at her clothes covered in paint.

"Go shower, I'll soak those." Stella smiled.

"How did I get…" Stella started to say. "Oh, daddy carried you to bed." Lilly sprung to her feet and smiled.

"Thank you." She said.

"You're welcome." I nodded.

"No time like the present!" Cassie elbowed me hard in the rib and I dropped to a knee.

"That's perfect." Lilly walked in front of me using her hands as a camera.

"Now Stella you stand here." Cassie pushed her in front of me as I rubbed my rib.

"What's happening?" Stella was confused as she chomped on the rest of her taco.

"Dad now!" Cassie ordered.

"Now, or you'll never do it." Lilly agreed.

"WAIT FOR ME!" Audrey climbed the stairs still un-showered but covered in a dry towel.

"Okay, go for it." She puffed.

"Shit…" I tried to stand up.

Lilly raced to my side and pushed me back down. "Stay there, it has a better effect." She whispered in my ear, and I smiled at my sweet girl.

"Stella…" I uttered.

"Yes, Dane." She tried not to laugh.

"Will you be my date for the Halloween dance?" I mumbled.

"Sorry, I couldn't hear you. Could you speak a little clearer?" She teased and giggled with the girls.

"WILL YOU PLEASE GO TO THE DANCE WITH ME!" I said loudly.

"Oh…" She smiled.

"WELL?" Cassie was impatient.

"Yes, I'd love to." Stella laughed.

"WOOOOOO!" Lilly clapped.

"By the way you owe the jar a dollar." Audrey winked at me.

"If you want dresses, I'm immune from the jar for a month." I offered my hand out to seal the deal.

"Fine, we shop tomorrow. No school." Audrey yawned.

"Deal, but we sleep in." I glared playfully.

"10 am…" She tried to negotiate.

"12?" I pressed.

"11 am and I'll make breakfast." Stella added.

"Done!" Audrey smiled.

"Can you make waffles?" Lilly asked.

"Not without a waffle iron." She apologized.

"Add that to the list." Lilly slapped the Lowe's shopping list into Audrey.

"Okay. Everyone to bed." I clapped my hands to get their attention.

"Yes! Mr. De La Roche." Cassie poked her tongue out.

The girls ran off downstairs and I retreated to the couch that had become my bed and quickly sent off an email to my boss and the administrators to let them all know we'd all be away for the day tomorrow.

Stella came over with two blankets and laid down on the other side of the couch while the girls piled into my bed.

Stella

I woke up a little earlier than the others and went outside with Tux to harvest the last of the veggies for the season. The mornings were getting chillier now. Pumpkins and carrots were the only things I was getting. The odd radish and there was one final cauliflower hanging on for dear life. The peach tree had dropped all its fruit now and all that was left was in the fridge.

It was a quaint home, so warm and welcoming. Just like the family who lived here.

I was excited for the girls to see their rooms. The rest of the week would be spent sticking rhinestones to dresses, making wings out of wire coat hangers and old stockings, and sewing tulle into skirts and I was secretly excited.

Ana and I had made a lot of our costumes as kids even if they didn't turn out so well. I'd planned flower crowns, and gold embellishments with butterflies and all things whimsy and fairytale.

Now that I was going, I had to have my own costume and as I cooked, I tried to brainstorm something unique, something colorful for the woodland theme.

It was almost 11 am and the smell of bacon woke Dane first and Tux trotted over to me and scored himself the first piece of bacon.

"Morning sunshine." I smiled and Dane stood up shirtless and stretched and flexed all his muscles in my direction.

I put my head down trying to ignore him and all of his perfection. I was hovering over a stove in a shirt four sizes too big, my hair in a messy bun on top of my head, odd socks on my feet, and I was pretty sure they weren't even my socks.

"Coffee?" Dane asked.

"Of course." I smiled as I poured a mug for him, he walked over to me and kissed my cheek to thank me for the coffee.

"Hey, are you still going as a faun?" I questioned.

Dane laughed and nodded. "Is that okay, do you want us to match? We can." He smiled.

"I don't mind, I don't know what to wear. I might just let the girls pick for me." I laughed.

"Don't make that mistake, they are hot and cold." He laughed back.

"Okay, I'll stick with the nymph." I smiled.

"Can I see the nymph in private after?" He smiled.

"We'll see." I brushed his beard with my fingers as his arms reached behind my back.

"We can't do that again." I whispered.

"I know, I just want one thing." He smirked.

"And what's that?" I asked.

"A kiss." He smiled.

I pressed up through my feet to try to match his height and kissed him softly.

His arms tightened around me, I dropped the spatula as I wrapped my arms around him, and he kissed down my neck gently and came to a sudden halt.

"CRAP!" He dropped me.

"Ouch!" I yelled as my tailbone hit the bench.

"OH. MY…"Cassie swooned, her hands clasped together, and she skipped around the room excitedly.

"I KNEW IT! She yelled.

"Cassie…" Dane tried to slow her down.

"What are you screaming about?" Audrey came out and rubbed her eyes.

"I saw them kissing!" She clapped.

"Probably not the first time." Audrey chuckled. My cheeks went red at Audrey's observations.

"It's totally fine. We want her to stay." Audrey followed.

"Guys, we aren't a thing. We just…ummmm." I froze mid-explanation.

"What Stella is trying to say is, that we do like each other a little more than friends, but we aren't rushing into anything. Neither of us is ready right now but sometimes when you're an adult it's nice to have another adult to keep you company." Dane said.

"And kiss?" Cassie smiled.

"Yes, and kiss." I admitted.

"Now you don't have to hide it from us." Audrey smiled.

"We don't do it a lot; this is the second time." Dane sighed.

"Third." I corrected him.

"Okay third but we aren't getting married. I know that's where your minds are going. Don't tell Lilly!" I ordered with a finger pointed between them both.

"Fine, but I want a crown." Cassie was trying to negotiate again.

"And what do I get if you slip up?" Dane asked.

"Dishes for a week." She offered her hand.

"A month?" I offered mine hesitantly, not ready to shake.

"Two weeks?" She said.

"Three?" I squinted.

"Fine." She smiled and grabbed my hand to shake it.

She ran off to google her crown and Audrey sat looking between me and Dane with these crazy eyes she only brought out when she was extremely excited or happy.

"You're scaring me." Dane laughed.

"You're happy, it makes me happy too." She hugged me first and then Dane and walked off to get dressed.

"FUCK!" He grasped the counter.

"They took it well." I encouraged.

"Too well, they'll be planning a honeymoon on the car ride to Lowes." Dane laughed.

"Well, that isn't happening." I said and realized how insensitive it sounded far too late. "Sorry, I spoke before I thought." I apologized.

"No, it's cool. Your position is firm, I haven't got any ideas to take you away from plans you already have." He said as he tried to fake a smile.

"I'll go get Lilly up." Dane was quick to change the subject and he yelled for Cassie and Audrey to come and start eating.

Cassie and Audrey helped me bring the plates of food to the table and they both sat beside me and glared at me from both sides.

"Okay, you're scaring me…" I backed my seat away, but Audrey wrapped her foot around the leg of my chair and held me there.

"Stella." Cassie grabbed my hand.

"Yes?" I shuddered in horror that they might hurt me.

"Please don't hurt him. It took a long time to get him to where he is now." Audrey said with a hint of threat in her voice. They'd had time to discuss this, and it was now apparent they would drown me in dishwater if I hurt Dane.

"Girls your dad and I have been very clear about what happens next, and he knows I'm only here a short time. You might get a stepmom someday, but it won't be me." I said softly.

"I read enough books to know how this goes…" Audrey rolled her eyes, and I felt the first wave of what it was like to feel her cold shoulder and I suddenly felt a little sorry for Gina.

Audrey had a way of making you feel so loved and cherished but now I was threatening her delicate balance of life, and it was a very loud red flag.

Cassie suddenly wasn't fun; she was a bodyguard and even though she was eight I knew she'd do her absolute best to make me feel physical pain if I caused any to Dane.

"I promise, no more funny business. Just work and helping around the house." My eyes begged them both.

"I think that's wise. He needs love right now and if you aren't staying let him find the real thing." Audrey's eyes locked mine and her wisdom was far beyond her years.

I never thought I'd be afraid of a bunch of kids, but here I was about to shit my pants.

Dane and Lilly walked in and sat on the opposite side of the table and Cassie and Audrey's demeanors changed immediately.

"Ready for some shopping?" Dane smiled.

"Sure." Cassie said shortly.

"Get excited. Stella is going to turn us into actual fairies!" Lilly beamed.

I laughed a little awkwardly and choked all at the same time. "I'll try." I smiled through my scrambled eggs.

"You got this." Cassie whacked me on the back softly.

"Thanks." I smiled at her.

Everyone ate mostly in silence except for Lilly and her odd questions.

Dane's phone rang and he walked off to his bedroom to answer it and took a few minutes while the girls ate a second serving of bacon and pancakes.

"Who was that?" Audrey asked as Dane walked back in.

"That was your mom." He said.

"Why?" Cassie asked.

"Not yours, hers." He smiled at me.

"Why are you talking to my mother?" I coughed.

"We're friends now." He smiled.

"That's so weird." I put my head down.

I knew Dane was up to something and it was all over Lilly's face, she knew a secret. We were all carrying extra weight right now and it all revolved around me, and I wanted to curl up and cry. Duluth was feeling like a really big mistake right about now.

"Mind if I sit this one out?" I'm not feeling so good." I said as I stood up to wash my dishes and collect the other empty plates.

"Yeah of course. Get some rest." Dane nodded.

I retreated to my van and sat in the tiny shower cabin like I did on every other really bad day. The tightness of the space made me feel secure, like I wouldn't fall over or do something wild.

Tux perched his head on my leg. Like always he knew when I wasn't doing so good. I'd ride a good wave for a while until something bumped me off and I was starting to feel that bump approaching.

"Let's hit the water." I said to Tux while I played with his ears.

I waited for Dane and the girls to leave and then I unhooked the van and headed back to the yacht club. I changed into some wet gear and put Tux's vest on, and I hauled the kayak to the bank of the water and like a million times before we climbed in and paddled out away from anywhere anyone could hurt me.

On the water, I was the only one who could do that. I was trapped with my own thoughts and for the first time it wasn't about Ana, but I so desperately wanted to tell her everything, I wanted to cry to her, I wanted to scream and kick and shout because she got it, she never judged, she just let me release and I'd do the same for her.

I felt so frozen in life. I wasn't moving forward; I was just standing still, and the world was moving around me. Sure, I traveled but the minute something felt too hard or too serious I packed up and left, and it was feeling hard now that the girls knew.

I think they underestimated what a relationship between Dane and I would look like and the minute it didn't fit their mold I wasn't enough.

I was meant to be there for them, to guide them through this already difficult phase of their lives and I managed to completely flip that into something that was all about me. I adored those girls, and I knew if my future was clearer, they'd welcome me with open arms, but I couldn't give anyone one hundred percent of me.

We'd been on the water a good long while now and the sunset began to change the sky to its orange, peachy tones and it glowed and simultaneously blinded me as Tux barked loudly at the shore.

"What's that?" I tried to calm him, but he continued to get rowdier with excitement.

"Stella!" A woman's voice called.

I knew that voice, but I hadn't heard it in a long time, not in real-time. The sunset was still blinding me as I rowed to the shore.

"Mom?" Tux was already out of the kayak and all over her.

Dane was in the truck behind her, and it was clear they had meant to surprise me. Dane called Tux over, so he'd get off of her.

"What are you doing here?" I raced over and hugged her tightly the second I climbed out of the kayak.

"I needed to see my girl." She brushed my hair back off my face.

Her face was a little more aged, she had a few more wrinkles and a few extra wiry white hairs than when I saw her last.

"You look good." She poked at me.

"I've missed you." I smiled.

"Yeah right, that's why you come home so often." She laughed.

"Where's dad?" I asked.

"He's at Dane's putting up a bookshelf and an office table and attached some new taps in the attic bedroom." She quizzed me.

"He can never sit still." I laughed.

Dane waved and took off back towards home leaving me alone with my mom.

I dragged the kayak over to my van and dried Tux off before he climbed into the van. Then I hoisted the kayak back onto the roof to secure it down and my mom watched from the side proudly.

"And you do this every day?" She smiled.

"Not every day. Maybe once a week." I answered.

"No wonder you're so fit." She watched me with proud eyes.

"Come on, I'd like to see dad." I ushered her into the passenger seat.

"I'm glad you're here actually. You can sew and those girls want fairy costumes I'm not sure I have the skills for." I sighed.

"Yes, you do, but I'm happy to help. They seem lovely." She played with my hair as I drove.

"I've missed this." I turned to her. She would always play with my hair and braid it when we watched movies together.

"When's the dance?" she asked.

"Next week." I replied.

"We have some work to do." She sighed.

"We do..." I agreed.

I drove into the long driveway once we reached the house and Dane was standing under the large trees ready to help me hook up the van.

I climbed down from the driver's seat, and he handed me the water hose.

"Thanks." I said as I took the hose.

"You, okay?" He whispered.

"I'm good." I nodded as I pulled away and opened the back sliding door for Tux.

"Dane, I do adore your home." Mom stood taking in the large trees.

"Thanks, Addy." Dane smiled.

"How's he doing up there?" Mom asked.

"He's almost done! Stella, you never told me how handy your father was." He was trying so hard to get more than a one worded response from me.

"Did you get some sheets for that room?" I asked.

"Yeah, they're on the bench." Dane sighed.

"See you guys inside." I walked off towards the front door where I could hear the girls playing 'Long Live'.

I grabbed the shopping bag and rushed past them as quickly as I could and headed for the laundry and I caught a   glimpse   of   them   all   dancing together. Audrey caught me in her frame, but I moved too fast for her to stop me, and I locked myself in the laundry and sank to the floor.

I sat there and unwrapped the different sizes of sheets slowly and unfolded them all so I could wash them, but I mostly used them as tissues for the first five minutes.

"Stell's?" It was Theo's voice, my father.

I unlocked the door and he poured into the room and squeezed me before he even looked at my face.

"Oh sweetheart, what's wrong?" He wiped my face with his dirty thumbs and kissed my forehead.

"I want to come home, but it doesn't feel like home anymore. And now this feels like home, but I can't be that person for them. And I feel *so* lost." I wept.

"You've been running a long time my girl." He hugged me. "And maybe that's my fault for telling you to go instead of letting you face your fears. I thought I was protecting you by sending you away." He patted my hair.

"You did and said all the right things. I just got carried away. But home isn't a place." I sighed.

"It's a feeling." Theo replied.

I nodded as I wiped my tears.

"I like him. If my opinion holds any value." He smiled.

"It's not him." I sighed.

"Then what?" He asked.

I couldn't answer him. I'd trapped myself in this pattern of stopping, starting, grieving a little, working, and getting close to absolutely nobody. I was so afraid of people hurting me that I didn't realize I was doing the hurting now.

"You can come home anytime and pick up where you left off." He said.

"I know, I'm just not done with this. I'm just having a moment of weakness. I have so much to see, Dad. I can't stop now." I took a deep breath.

"The offer stands indefinitely." He smiled and I hugged him one more time.

I wasn't sure what was up with Stella, but I knew something was off and I had a feeling I knew who to ask, I made a beeline for Cassie and Audrey after excusing myself from Addy who was inspecting the flowers along the pathway that were there when I bought the house.

"You two… come here." I waved them over with a serious index finger and they both froze.

Lilly was confused and shrugged her shoulders as she continued her own personal concert singing in the lounge room.

I took them out the back and they leaned against the wall and didn't make eye contact with me.

"What did you say?" I asked calmly.

They looked at each other and kept quiet, sticking together like true sisters do.

"Well, someone's going to tell me, or I'll paint your rooms black, and you'll have milk crates for furniture." I crossed my arms and waited for someone to comply.

"We just warned her not to hurt you." Audrey took responsibility and spoke up first.

"We were a little threatening. Sorry, we just don't want to see you hurt again like when mom left you." Cassie explained.

"She left *us*. We're a package deal." Audrey rolled her eyes.

"And she didn't take it too well." I sighed.

"She gets it, she said you guys had already talked about it." Cassie questioned.

"Yes, we did. Which is why kids should butt out." I glowered.

"Dad!" Audrey growled.

I peeked an eyebrow and waited for her to say what was really on her mind.

"You guys might think kissing and cuddling is all fun and cute, but somebody always gets hurt." Audrey elaborated.

"Maybe I shouldn't let you read so many books." I yawned.

"Don't cry to me when you can't peel yourself off the bathroom floor AGAIN!" She raced inside and slammed the door and went to her room.

I followed in behind her and she burst into tears at the sight of her room.

"Woah!" Cassie said from behind me as she smiled at the windowsill reading nook fit for a princess.

"This is beautiful…" She said as she walked around the room taking in all the details and decorations that Stella had added for her.

"What do you think?" I asked.

"I love it." She smiled.

Stella stood in the doorway and smiled as she watched Audrey taking in the chandelier that Theo had just installed as a reading light over the window and Addy had arranged all her books onto the shelves by color. Her bed was finally made properly, and it looked much more complete than when she first saw it.

Audrey ran to Stella and hugged her and held on as she wept joyfully into her.

"I'm sorry, I   blamed   you   for   what   Mom did and I shouldn't have done that. You've been nothing but wonderful to all of us." Stella wiped her eyes and pulled her hair off her face and a tear escaped Stella's eye.

"No, you had every right. Look, there is no doubt it'll be hard when I leave. But maybe that feeling means we cared enough to let it hurt. You know I'm only a phone call away if you ever need me. And I hope if I ever need you, you'll answer my calls?" Stella brushed her cheeks.

Audrey nodded and squeezed Stella a little tighter. "I don't want you to go." Cassie cried as she slammed into her and Audrey and joined the hug.

"I'm not leaving for a while." Stella hugged her back.

"Well, this is sweet and all but I'm hungry." Lilly ran to the bedroom and froze as she looked around.

"Can I see mine?" She screamed as she looked around, but before we could answer she had run to her room already and busted through the door startling Addy.

Addy was in there fixing the sheets onto the bed and packing away her clothes and Lilly tugged at Addy's hand and smiled as she thanked her for helping.

"This is a very beautiful room for a beautiful young lady." Addy smiled as she showed her the fairies on each wall.

"Okay, my turn!" Cassie smirked and turned to her door, closed her eyes, and stepped inside.

She counted to three, opened her eyes, and screamed almost louder than Lilly when she saw her four-posted bed and the vines hanging from the roof.

"This is insane!" She jumped up and down.

"What's insane is I can sleep in my own bed tonight." I yawned as Addy came in with extra blankets for Cassie.

"Did you finish the attic?" Stella asked me.

"Your dad did." I smiled.

"Dane said we can sleep upstairs if that's okay with you." Addy smiled.

"Of course." Stella nodded.

"Okay, now costumes!" Cassie pulled Addy to the couch and unloaded the bag of dresses, tulle, beads, rhinestones, and glitter beside Addy.

"After dinner maybe. Addy's probably tired." I shook my head.

"Lucky I'm handy with a needle and thread." Addy held up the dresses one by one and glanced pleasingly at Stella who was perched on the other side of the couch.

It was apparent where Stella got her good nature and handiness from. Her parents were proactive and always doing things, they seemed to have talents pouring from their fingers. Stella had all the good parts of Addy and Theo thrown into one.

Addy wasted no time. She had the girls gluing rhinestones onto their dresses and coaching Theo as he attempted to stitch on sequins.

"At this rate, we'll be done by tomorrow!" Lilly beamed.

"We aren't going all night." I laughed as I threaded tulle onto wire coat hangers as I watched a tutorial on how to make fairy wings. For each set I finished Cassie would then add glitter.

"Let's put on a movie." Stella hopped up to stretch as she shuffled through an old folder with DVDs.

"Good idea, if I hear Cruel Summer one more time…" I muttered.

"Don't finish that sentence." Audrey snarled playfully.

"It's annoyingly catchy, that's all. I'm always singing it at school." I laughed.

"I'm yet to see that." Stella giggled.

"Does everyone like Beauty and the Beast?" Stella asked.

"LOVE!" Audrey smiled.

"No other votes are necessary." Stella winked as she started the movie and sat done to resume bejeweling dresses.

Addy had sewn in layers upon layers of tulle creating extravagant ballgown-style dresses but short enough that they wouldn't drag along the floor. Theo had given up and was engrossed in the movie until his stomach started to grumble.

"Let's leave the girls and go grab some food, maybe some beers." Theo smacked me on the shoulder.

"Yes please, sir." I stood up and grabbed my keys and the girls barely noticed us moving.

Stella was measuring Cassie for elastic that would secure her wings while Lilly danced around in her dress that was finished.

Theo and I walked out to the car and Tux came along with us. I helped him up into the truck and he seemed relieved to be away from all of the noise.

"I don't know how you do it with three girls, Dane." Theo said admirably.

"Honestly it wouldn't have been so easy without Stella. She swept in one day and just took control and I've been sidelined ever since." I confessed.

"She sees people in need and she gives her all." Theo smiled.

"I'll be lost when she leaves us." I sighed.

"If she leaves." Theo grinned as he stroked Tux's long coat.

"I've offered, but she's on a mission and I can't get in her way." I explained.

"She's fond of you, and I can see how much she adores the girls. But I know she wants to finish." Theo grunted.

"It's important to her, I respect that." I smiled.

"She'll be at this the rest of her life if we let her. It wasn't meant to be four years and only six states. It was meant to be a year or two and all forty-eight then fly to the rest." Theo seemed to disapprove now.

"You and Addy worry…" I empathized.

"Like you would if it were your girls." He nodded.

I tried to imagine one or all of my girls out in the world at that age and the idea made my stomach do backflips. Not everyone is kind, not every situation is warm and inviting, and there are real dangers out there that I wouldn't be able to protect them from.

"It's horrifying, isn't it?" He looked me in the eye as we pulled up to traffic lights.

We were both military men and had seen things unimaginable. But we didn't need to talk about that, we just knew.

"For as long as she wants to stay, I'll look after her." I promised him.

"How has she been?" Theo quizzed me, but I knew what he meant.

"Ana?" I asked.

He nodded with a deep breath.

"Some days it hurts more than others. She still kayaks alone and works it out on the water, then when she's back on land she's back to business." I explained.

"I thought as much, she's always been so poised. She used to be so confident you could never tell her what to do. She always knew what she wanted in life and now she's conflicted, I guess that's her new normal." Theo sighed.

His eyes welled a little as he turned to the window, and I could see the glimmer of a tear in the reflection of the window. Ana wasn't just Stella's friend; she was family to all of them.

"You lost both of them…" I remarked and I noticed his heart sink the minute I said those words and he strived to compose himself.

"It was a horrible accident. I'll never forget the scream Stella let out when she got the phone call. She screamed for days until she made herself so sick that the sound wouldn't come out anymore. Completely inconsolable, and then she was quiet. Stella wasn't a quiet child and I truly worried we'd lose her too." He confessed.

"I can't imagine what it would be like to see your child suffering like that." I sighed.

"Your girls remind me of them when they were youngsters. Fighting, playing, singing, dancing, they did everything together." Theo smiled at the memory of it all.

"And god forbid if they turn on you." I laughed trying to lift the mood.

"All the training in the world couldn't save me." I chuckled.

Theo laughed aloud as we pulled up to a pizza shop.

We both got out of the car and cracked the windows for Tux. Once inside I ordered four large pizzas and Theo went next door to buy drinks for the girls and beers for us.

Once we arrived home the girls were all dancing around in their new dresses, fairy wings, and tiaras while Stella and her mom were making the bed upstairs.

"I'm hungry!" Lilly raced to me and grabbed a pizza off the top of the stack before I could place them down on the new dining table that had arrived with the mattresses.

"Cass, get some plates please." I said as she approached with her nose out first.

"Lilly! Change your clothes before you start eating, that goes for all of you!" Stella said as she raced down the stairs.

I cracked a beer and held it out for her, she obliged and took a swig before handing it back to me.

I sunk into the chair closest to me and Stella sat beside me, her parents sat down at the other end of the long table affectionately chattering while we waited for the girls to come back out in their normal clothes.

Stella opened all the boxes, flipped the lids underneath the boxes, and moved the stack of plates to the center of the table.

"Okay, let's eat!" Audrey said as she pulled out a chair and claimed some slices of the pepperoni pizza.

Lilly and Cassie soon followed behind and soon we were all eating the square-cut slices of pizza. Audrey was always after the slices with the most crust, while Cassie only wanted the middle pieces.

"They are a good team!" Addy remarked and Audrey cleaned Cassie's plate of crusts.

"I eat both. I'm superior." Lilly smiled.

"You were the final edit." Stella added.

"Are you saying we are drafts?" Cassie smirked at Stella.

"Well, yes. I suppose I am." She laughed.

"Then what were you?" Audrey asked her.

"Oh, I didn't need a draft, they got it right the first time around." Stella teased.

Addy rolled her eyes playfully and continued eating her pizza.

"How long are you staying?" Cassie asked Theo.

"Just till Thursday." He replied.

"You'll miss the dance!" She frowned.

"Dad and Stella will have to send us lots of photos. You can FaceTime us if you want to." Addy suggested.

"Can we?" Lilly said excitedly.

"Of course!" Stella said through a mouthful of food.

"Can we wear makeup, daddy?" Cassie fluttered her lashes at me.

Makeup, I dreaded this moment. Soon my bathroom would be covered in foundation, pink lipstick, and blue eyeshadow, and I was helpless to stop it. It was just the natural order of how things were going to be. I suppose I had done well to avoid it this long. The girls in Audrey's class were always experimenting with all sorts of wild colors on their lips and eyes.

"I suppose so." I said through the last mouthful of my beer.

Stella looked at me and snickered as she cracked a second beer and handed it to me.

"Keep 'em coming." I winked.

She kicked me from underneath the table and I flinched and spilled the full beer on my plate of pizza and over my chest.

"Shit." I hissed.

"Sorry!" Stella apologized as she ran to the kitchen for paper towels, and I followed behind her.

"It's fine, settle down." I laughed as Stella raced around freaking out.

I pulled off my shirt and wrung it out in the kitchen sink.

"Go shower." She turned to me and closed her eyes suddenly. She was trying not to look at my naked chest.

I stood in front of her laughing ignoring her command until she wet the tip of a tea towel and threatened me with it.

"Now Dane!" She giggled as she gently flicked me with it.

"Haven't you learned not to flirt with me from that mess you just created?" I teased.

"Give me the shirt. Go shower!" She growled softly.

Addy was cleaning up the table and Stella brought the bin over to her and dumped the soggy pizza and wet paper towels into it as I strolled to the bathroom and locked myself inside.

I undressed and rinsed the beer from my clothes in the sink and took the time to trim my ever-growing beard just enough to look tidy when I rocked up to work tomorrow.

As I left the bathroom, I could hear Theo reading the girls a story. Stella and Addy seemed to be unpacking the kitchen, something I had dreaded doing for months.

In the laundry, there was a pile of dirty clothes and linens that seemed to be organized into piles. One for adult clothes, one for kids, one for towels, and the last for linens. Most were not big enough to be thrown into the machine until I dumped my pile on top. I opened the washer and dumped the pile of adult clothes with a cap full of detergent and a cap full of everything else Stella had perfectly organized on the shelf in front of me.

The dryer had a load of finished towels, and I pulled them out and folded them. Stella appeared in the corner of my eye, and she slumped against the door frame with a grin.

"I was getting to that." She whispered.

"I am perfectly capable." I winked.

She had armfuls of new tea towels spilling over her forearms. She placed them down into a pile of their own, gave me a gentle but not flirty grin, and walked back up the hallway toward the kitchen.

I followed but detoured to my bedroom to change out of the towel that I had wrapped around my waist.

In the kitchen, Addy was stacking the dishwasher with utensils that had lived in boxes for months. Stella was breaking boxes and dragging them through the formal dining area into the front lounge room that nobody ever even went into.

"Why have I never been in here?" Stella gasped.

I followed her into the formal dining room and switched on another light.

"It's just too much space to clean." I laughed.

"I guess so. It would be nice lit up with all the fixings." She swooned.

In her head, I knew she was seeing candlesticks and silverware, linen napkins, and expensive wines. It was a beautiful room after all. It was different from the rest of the house. It had an old dusty chandelier, ornamental plastering on the ceiling and the walls were a dark shade of navy blue. All it needed was a nice dining table and a posh rug.

"One day." I sighed.

"Think of all the tea parties." She giggled.

"you'll have to stick around for that." Addy said as she popped her head over Stella's shoulder and winked at me.

"Or I could come back for a visit." She wrapped her arm around Addy's hip and hugged her.

Addy sucked in a deep breath and exhaled loudly, as she rested her head on Stella's shoulder.

Stella rolled her eyes playfully and dropped her hand and walked out to the lounge where Theo was reading the girls 'The Hobbit'. Lilly and Cassie were yawning, their eyes heavy. Audrey was hanging onto his every word.

Lilly's eyes became heavier, and I lifted her from the couch and carried her to her bedroom. Stella was putting on a nightlight where she held up an empty plastic sleeve labeled with 'waterproof' mattress protector to assure me her new mattress would be safe from any accidents since she hadn't made it to the bathroom before falling asleep.

Stella tucked her in while I ushered Cassie to the toilet before she scurried off to her new room.

"Can we just finish this chapter?" Audrey begged as I zeroed in on her next.

"There's only two more pages." Theo smiled.

"Straight to bed after. I'm going to crash." I kissed her head and said goodnight to Theo.

Stella was upstairs with Addy, and I slipped away to my bedroom and sunk into the cold blankets for the first time in a long time, alone. It was weird not to be sleeping in the lounge room, but it was a welcome change. This room was large but cozy. The laundry baskets didn't take up the only free space anymore, but there were still boxes of belongings that I didn't seem to miss. Boxes of memories I didn't care to remember.

I heard the girls stomping through the house as they ran off to bed and the house became quiet after Theo climbed the stairs.

Stella

I hadn't realized how much I missed my parents. The first night they were here I slept with my mom and clung to her while my dad slept on an air mattress with Tux in the same room.

The days with them went too quickly, every spare moment we had we spent beading and gluing jewels and sequins onto costumes I no longer recognized. This was what I loved about my mom, her creativity, her generosity with her time, her bottomless pit of love she had for strangers, and the way she made everyone feel like she was their safe place. I wanted so much to be like her as a kid. She embodied a grace too timeless for me to grasp, too out of reach. I caught myself staring at her and just taking her in and really packing these memories away.

My dad spent his days doing odd jobs around the house, he had a lot of time for Dane. They would take Tux for walks each evening after he finished work. Mom thought it was cute they had struck up such a good friendship, and

Dad even offered to change the oil in the truck while he did mine which Dane obliged.

"I was thinking we might extend our stay…" Mom smiled as she mixed chives into her warm potato salad.

"If that's okay?" She added hesitantly.

"YESSS!" Cassie squealed from across the living room.

I laughed without breaking the seal of my lips and dipped my chin as I nodded still smiling while Cassie pulled herself up on the bench.

"This is perfect! You can come to the dance." She clapped.

"Would I be allowed?" Mom asked.

"The seamstress deserves to be the guest of honor." She gleamed.

"What will I wear?" Mom said animatedly.

"Oh! We should get you a dress too." Lilly walked over interested in the food as I chopped up bacon, shallots, and cappers.

"It's your day off tomorrow? Thrift shopping?" She turned to me.

"Sure!" I agreed.

"Can we have the day off?" Audrey asked as she sat herself next to Cassie.

"Help me up!" Lilly hit Audrey playfully.

"No, this is a rite of passage." She poked her tongue at Lilly.

Cassie giggled but helped pull her up as I turned her around and gave her a slight lift.

"No, you have to go to school." I sighed. "Unless your dad says otherwise…" I winked.

"DADDY!" Cassie screamed.

"Ugh, Cass! You have some good pipes on you." I rubbed my ears.

"How can I help?" Dane popped in through the back door.

"We can't go to school tomorrow…" Audrey shrugged her shoulders.

"And why would that be?" He seemed less than impressed.

"Because Addy and Theo are staying for the dance, and we need to take them thrift shopping for an outfit." Cassie explained.

"We are?" Dad questioned.

"I was speculating, that's all." Mom laughed.

"You are welcome to stay longer." Dane smiled.

"Thank you." Mom said.

"I'll call the airline. We have to be back Monday though; I have a fishing trip with Brian." Dad explained.

The sound of Brian's name was like salt in an open wound. Brian was Ana's dad; He and my dad had become good friends during our childhood and maintained that closeness even after her passing.

Before I even knew what my body was doing, I was walking out the front door to my van, I locked myself inside and lay on the bed on top of the blankets as I stared blankly at the ceiling. Enough time passed and I realized I had been asleep for quite a while. When I peered outside the lights through the house were off and I climbed under blankets and checked my phone.

The was one message from Dane.

If you need to talk, you
know where to find me.

That was hours ago and probably a few awkward conversations later.

The air was crisp and kept me awake. I pulled on my wetsuit and some warmer clothes and quietly unhooked the van and drove off down to the yacht club.

I knew I should have been better at this by now, why wasn't I? Why was I stuck in the same loop over and over again? I was so aware of how bad I was in these moments; I would glaze over and almost black out and completely freeze. I craved the water; it was the only thing that healed me. It was the only place I felt connected. Like all the water or tears filled up all the holes I had in me. It was rough, one minute I was doing better and then I wasn't.

This grief was relentless, I never wanted to feel this way over losing anyone else ever again. I wouldn't survive, I felt too much.

I pulled the kayak down and for the first time, I realized I didn't have Tux. He was probably snoring peacefully on the couch inside the house, or on the bed upstairs with my parents, maybe sleeping with Dane in his oversized bed.

I clipped on my life vest, screwed my oar together and pushed the kayak out, and climbed in when I saw the lights of a vehicle pull up next to my van. I couldn't see too much in the dark, but I heard the bark. Tux!

He kept barking as he raced to the kayak with his life vest on and leaped in with me. I wasn't sure who drove him down, but it made me feel a lot more put together knowing he was with me.

We paddled down past the lighthouse and back again. We had been gone at least an hour, maybe longer. When we got back to the yacht club Dane's truck was still running, the lights still on and I pulled the kayak onto the bank with Tux's help as he pulled a rope.

I peered my head into the truck and my dad was asleep with the seat reclined and a blanket thrown over him. Mom was in the passenger seat also asleep, and another blanket was thrown over her.

"Hey! Go home." I shrugged them gently.

"Oh shit! How long have you been standing here?" My dad shrieked.

"Not long. Thanks for bringing Tux, you should have gone back to the house though, you don't need to wait for me." I thanked them as Mom rubbed her eyes.

"We couldn't just leave you alone out here in the dark." Mom yawned.

"The Coast Guard is right there." I pointed.

"Still..." Mom yawned a little more.

"I'm sorry Stell, I didn't mean to upset you." My dad whispered softly.

"It's more a me thing, than a *you thing*. I'm okay." I assured him.

"You need to come home..." Mom sighed. Her expression was sadness and defeat.

"You know I can't do that." I whispered under my breath.

"You're wasting your life, Stella. It's time to stop this nonsensical life you're living and do something worthwhile." Dad growled back.

I froze and went back to my van where I loaded the kayak and dried Tux off. Dad sped out of the car park, and I was shocked that he had said that. He was never harsh, not like that.

Mom stood there in the dark, the moonlight caught her kind blue eyes. I hadn't even heard her door open and close, but I felt her presence. Ever warm and empathetic.

She climbed into the van and Tux rested his head in her lap as I climbed into the driver's seat. I took a deep breath and sat back in the chair with no intent on driving.

"He's not wrong." I hissed through my teeth.

"He is, and he isn't." She reached for my hand.

"I'm so scared mom." My eyes welled as my voice caught in my throat.

"Life stopped for all of us, but it never restarted for you. You are just lost, blowing through the wind, and that's okay for a time. But Estella, I think you've found something wonderful here, you are better around them. Dane is captivated by you, and you come alive in his presence. You have such a way about you and those little girls need you." Tears streamed down her face.

"I don't know how to be a mom…" I sniffed.

"That's okay, you do know how to be a friend." She brushed the wet hair off my face.

"I'm not ready for any of this. I don't know if I ever will." I added.

"Then decide before you break more hearts than your own." She pressed.

I started the engine and headed back to the house. The drive was eerily quiet as she shut off the radio.

Dane was sitting in the driveway on the ground as I pulled in and Addy leaped out and headed straight for the house.

I parked the van and Dane climbed into the passenger seat.

"Are you okay?" he asked with his head lowered, he didn't make eye contact.

"I need to leave…" I said softly.

"I know." He sighed.

"It's what I do." I grumbled.

"When will you go?" He sighed.

"After the dance. Is that okay? I'd love to see the girls dressed up." I asked.

"Of course, I can't braid hair." Dane smiled.

"In another life, maybe." I sighed.

"I know, ditto." He nodded.

"Have you heard from Gina?" I asked.

"She threatens me in texts on days I only presume she's fighting with James. She'll never follow through after her confrontation with the girls." He replied.

"If you ever need a character witness…" I raised my brows and smiled.

"I appreciate that." He replied.

"Did my dad say much?" I asked.

"More rambling, he has his opinions on the situation. He's entitled to those; doesn't mean you have to pay any attention. You are an adult, you can do what you want when you want." He said supportively.

"Is that what you would say to Audrey?" I asked.

"Absolutely not." He laughed.

I laughed with him and unbuckled my belt.

"For what it's worth, I'll be sad to see you go. You really did save me in a time when I was drowning." He confessed.

"Literally, I want weekly updates on the laundry situation. I worked hard at that." I laughed.

"I might have to keep your parents." He joked.

"You're doing great, you don't need help." I assured him.

"I don't know my daughter's, Stella. They are so grown up. It feels like I blinked, and they weren't in diapers anymore. They have these huge personalities and I'm still getting to know them. I spent so much time fixing worldly problems or teaching other people's kids. I forgot I needed to get to know my own kids." He sighed.

"And the best way to do that is with one-on-one time, you guys have so much more in common than you think." I smiled.

"You think?" he asked.

"I do." I smiled again.

"I'll miss you, Stella. Who is going to restock the hygiene drawers for me." He laughed.

"I'll be a phone call away if you ever need me to talk you through hair braiding." I laughed.

This felt good, it felt wholesome. I was taking a step, but it felt like a leap. Now that I knew what I was doing, I could prepare myself.

Dane

The next few days passed by quicker than I had liked. Addy and Theo had left and stuck to their original itinerary after the confrontations between Stella and her dad. They were back on good terms, but Addy wanted us to have the last few days to ourselves with the girls.

It was the day of the dance and Stella had spent her day off in the auditorium of the school setting up props, lighting, and decorations. She came home after 4 pm and I had homemade burgers and fries ready to go for everyone before they got dressed so we didn't end up with a sauce stain on any fairies.

"Okay, I'm getting dressed!" Cassie announced as she stuffed the last of her fries eagerly into her mouth.

"SAME!" Lilly followed her. Half a burger was still uneaten on the table.

Audrey was barely eating and spent most of the time pushing food around on the paper.

"I'm not hungry, dad." Audrey sighed.

"Are you feeling, okay?" I asked.

"Sure…" She grunted as she pushed her chair away from the table and she walked slowly down the hallway.

Stella pushed her way through the front door with a bouquet of flowers in her teeth and bags of makeup and accessories.

She opened her mouth to release the flowers onto the table and looked around worried. "Where are the girls?" she asked a little panicked.

"Getting dressed." I took the bags from her.

"Phew!" she smiled.

She picked up the flowers again and beelined for the bathroom and I heard the girls scream as they opened the bag of makeup.

I glared unwillingly at the costume Addy had put together for me and I dreaded wearing it tonight. The pants were fur, and it had an open chest vest that I knew was pushing the limits, so I pinned it shut with a safety pin.

"I look ridiculous…" I jumped into the doorway of the bathroom.

Cassie laughed as Lilly hugged me and Audrey rolled her eyes playfully as she swiped on a layer of glittery pink lipstick. She looked so grown up. Stella had curled her hair and sprayed it with glitter. Cassie had her hair up in a high loose bun, waves framing her face, and gold glitter on her cheekbones. Lilly had colorful hair extensions braided into her hair and a more natural makeup look.

I'd never seen Stella with this much makeup on. It was almost too much in the sense that I didn't recognize this version of her. She was almost too polished for the woman I had known.

The girls all helped each other pull on their dresses and Stella added the flowers by pinning them on their dresses and finally adding their wings she had covered in a reflective material, each embroidered with golden butterflies and leaves, and the mounds of glitter I had glue on with spray adhesive.

She snapped photos of us all together and then ran off to dress herself and the girls followed. When she appeared again, she was in a green dress that had flowers sewn into the waist and vines wrapping around her. Leaves and fake branches shaped her body and now her hair was down and covering her shoulders.

"You all look beautiful." I smiled as Stella poked at the safety pin.

"I'm not brave enough." I laughed.

"Maybe after a few fruit punches." She poked out her tongue.

It was nice to see her playful side coming out. She had been so focused on her next stop these last few days that we had seemed to just pass each other like two ships in the night.

"Let's go!" I ordered.

The girls excitedly ran for the front door. Audrey had perked up a little but stayed close to Stella.

Saying bye to Tux was a feeling I wasn't fond of. He had become such a good buddy to me. Our goodbyes were now limited.

"See you after." I hugged him.

The girls were already halfway down the street. Cassie had made comments on how she refused to crinkle her dress. She was gunning for the best-dressed prize, little to her knowledge I had entered them as a trio, so I didn't have to deal with tears from Lilly if Cassie won. Flora, Fauna, and Merryweather but with a lot more glitz and glamour. They all glimmered as they did a fast walk back to school.

Elderly neighbors smiled over at us from behind their pot plants and cups of tea from their front porches. Other homes full of kids raced out to walk with us to the school for the nightly festivities.

Once we reached the school the gates were decorated with pumpkins, fake webs, and witches' hats. The school principal was there to greet everyone, and some parents hung about as their children waited for friends.

The music inside was loud and Mark was hovering over an old DJ system.

"Side hustle I don't know about?" I questioned.

"Once upon a time, I had different aspirations in life." He laughed. "And now I DJ the school discos…" he sighed.

"We've all been there." I slapped him on the back.

"And what was yours?" He asked.

I pulled my vest to the side and on my chest, I had a faded tattoo of a frog skeleton holding a triton.

"That's why you're so ripped. I knew you weren't the typical schoolteacher build." He laughed.

"You knew I was in the force?" I question.

"Yeah, but I didn't know you were a frog." He shook my hand. "Thank you for your service." He said proudly.

I smiled back and took a swig of my fruit punch as I thought about what that service had cost me in life. It all brought me right back to this moment. My three beautiful little girls dancing without a care in the world.

Stella was talking with Audrey and her friends, and some of the teachers Stella had become friendly with.

I was on my seventh pizza roll when I knew it was getting late and I had to take a risk and ask Stella to dance. I'd already danced with each of the girls and Mark's company wasn't so great when he had every single mom hanging off him like flies to honey. He was dressed as Dracula and the jokes were dry and overused. I had been lucky enough to acquire a second safety pin from a tablecloth and kept myself off the principal's radar for most of the night.

"Okay, I'm going in." I flushed and handed Mark my drink.

"You got this." He winked as he browsed through his playlist.

I walked over to where Stella was eating a hotdog at a table with the girls and their friends, and I offered my hand, and she smiled as we connected, I pulled her up and I winked at the girls as they swooned.

Mark played 'The Man Who Can't Be Moved' and the whole room of people paired up and joined us on the dance floor.

I nodded as I resonated with the lyrics of the song and stared deeply into Stella's eyes.

"Thank you, Stella. You gave our family a heartbeat again." I smiled.

"It's been a pleasure getting to know you all." She sniffed as she dropped her head.

I pulled her into my chest and wrapped my arms tightly around her back and she rested her hands around my neck. Tears streamed silently down her cheeks and the girls noticed and quickly ran over to hug us.

I released her from my grasp and let the girls have her as I watched over them and Mark handed me another cup of punch.

"I heard she resigned." He sighed.

"Yeah…" I nodded.

"I'm here for you, all of you. It can't be easy on the girls." He empathized.

"Audrey's taking it the hardest." I said.

"It's a lot of change." He whispered.

I nodded in agreement and walked over to Lilly and grabbed her hand.

The dance floor was clearing as people were starting to leave. Stella and the other staff members started to pull down decorations and pack food away.

She was hugging people goodbye and exchanging pleasantries knowing she might not see them again. The principal wished her well and thanked her for her hard work and offered her a glowing report for future job references which she seemed thrilled for.

I walked the girls home and got them showered and ready for bed while Stella stayed at the school a few hours longer. It was the next day when I saw her again. She was fresh-faced and cooking breakfast.

Stella

It was odd to think this would be my last time cooking in this house, I wasn't fond of the idea, but I was excited for the next chapter. I had plans to see a little of Wisconsin before heading to Chicago and then making a sprint to Florida hopeful to skip a freezing cold winter.

Tux knew. He was sniffing around my overly stuffed bag and toiletry bag a little too much and made sounds that you would imagine a sad dog made. The huffs, puffs, and occasional whines. That seemed to stave off a little when I tossed him bacon or sausage.

Dane was the first one up and I presented him with a black coffee and a full plate of food that he seemed to push around the plate the way Audrey usually would if it was something she found unappetizing.

"Do you have accommodation sorted?" Dane asked.

"There's an RV park I've booked into at White Bear Lake. It's only about two hours from here." I replied.

"Don't suppose you want to stay for an early dinner then?" He asked.

I smiled softly as I considered it.

"You don't have to, just a thought." He added quickly.

"I'd love to." I smiled.

He finally started to eat the food and I sat across from him and did the same. The girls came out of their rooms looking like they'd been partying all night long and wrestled for the next interesting box of cereal.

"Dad, can you set up the tripod!" Cassie barked.

"It's Saturday, chop, chop people. We have subscribers to feed." Lilly clapped as she held the box of Weetabix with a letter taped to it.

Dane rushed around and set up the tripod and camera and the girls brushed through each other's hair quickly and had their bowls ready and the carton of milk.

"Hi everyone!" Cassie announced.

Audrey and Lilly waved to the camera while Cassie opened the box and did a sniff test. Lilly pulled off the letter and read it aloud to the camera and thanked the boy named Collin who had mailed it over for them and they soon cut to pouring the cereal.

"Oo, this is in the shape of a brick." Lilly was intrigued.

"They should have called it 'Weetabrix.'" Audrey giggled.

I couldn't help but chuckle a little to myself at her joke.

Cassie put a serving in her bowl and went to pour some milk when Lilly stopped her.

"It says to add hot water…" she gulped.

"Sorry folks, we seem to have a miscommunication." Cassie's eyes bulged.

"What?" Audrey snatched the letter.

"For kids, it says to add hot water…" She explained.

Dane rushed to the kitchen and boiled some water behind the girls and in the meantime, Cassie tried it with cold milk.

"That's' not food." She spat it out.

"Thanks Collin…" Lilly grinned cheekily and gave a sarcastic thumbs-up at the camera.

The water was boiling now, and Dane poured some over another serving and wished them luck.

"Stella is our honorary live-in nanny slash friend. It's only right she goes first." Audrey motioned for me to go over to them.

I was not ready for this, but I fixed myself up as quickly as I could, took a seat between the girls, and inhaled a big breath as I stared into the bowl that looked like vomit.

"You got this!" Lilly whispered in my ear.

"Here goes nothing." I squinted as I used a spoon to move the now soggy log of Weetabix around the bowl.

I raised a small spoon to my mouth and tried to be forgiving with my testing, but it was vile, and I spat it back out into my hand and jumped up and ran to the sink while the girls laughed at me.

"Your next." I pointed playfully as they swallowed their laughter and gawked down at the bowl.

"Youngest first." Audrey glared at Lilly.

One by one they reluctantly tested the cereal and each and every one spat it out and ran for the bathroom.

Dane came over and tried to save the video by reading through the letter once more and discovered Lilly had left out crucial steps.

"You're supposed to add sugar or honey." He snickered as he reached for the bottle of honey, swirled a generous amount over the sludge, and brought a spoon up to his mouth.

"That's not that bad." He added.

"Well, I'm glad you like it, that's your breakfast for a week! We've lost the cook." Lilly giggled into the camera.

The girls ended the video with a request for comments on what to try next and then shut off the camera.

"If I ever meet Collin." Audrey grumbled.

"He's British and probably has a fancy accent and posh hairdo. Audrey, you'll be swept off your feet before you can clench your fist." Dane teased.

Audrey's cheeks flushed and she smiled widely at the thought of it.

"In other news. Stella is staying for an early dinner. Any suggestions?" He asked.

"Chinese!" Cassie begged.

"I haven't had Chinese in years, let's do it." I smiled.

"Why haven't you had it in so long?" Lilly questioned.

"I haven't had anyone to share all the different dishes with." I said sadly.

"But you have Tux, I bet he could eat all of it." Cassie said as she played with his fluffy ears.

"He probably could!" I agreed.

"Okay, last day with Stella, but it's raining. What's the plan?" Dane asked.

"Pillow fort, movies, and hair braiding." Cassie was already hauling her blankets and pillows into the lounge.

"This one!" Lilly raced over with a DVD of 'The Sound of Music'.

Dane was organizing the pillows and blankets into sections for each of us while I ruffled through the cupboards for popcorn and snacks.

Audrey was washing the dishes and she seemed to have tears in her eyes.

I took the sponge from her hands, dried them with a tea towel, and led her into the dining room.

"Are you okay?" I whispered.

She didn't say a word but nodded against her will, we both knew she wasn't okay.

"Can I have a hug?" I asked.

She nodded once more, and I gently pulled her in for a hug and squeezed her trying to remember her warmth.

"You're really leaving." She sniffed into the mess our hair had become.

"Yeah, it's time for me to move on to the next town. You can call me as much as you want!" I wiped the tears off her cheeks.

My own eyes began to fill with tears as I looked into her beautiful wet face. I sat on the ground against the wall, and she sat in my lap, and I held her as she cried.

I didn't know how to fix this. I knew I was getting attached to them, and that's why I had to leave, but I didn't realize just how much they would miss me, they had each other, they weren't meant to miss me this much. My mom was right, I was breaking more hearts than my own. But I'd been broken for so long I didn't know how to leave anything whole.

Dane peered in from the kitchen leaned into the doorframe and crossed his arms across his chest as he let out a sigh and scrunched his face around as he looked over at Audrey with concern.

I looked up and mouthed 'sorry' at him and he nodded softly, and he leaned down to Audrey, and she clawed at him to hug her.

"Come on baby girl, let's go watch a movie." He picked her up and walked out of the dining room.

I pulled myself up, wiped off my face, and snuck off to the bathroom to clean up.

Dane followed behind me and we were facing off in the bathroom now.

"I should leave, I shouldn't drag this out." A tear dropped to my cheek.

"You have to do what you think is right, Stella. I can't tell you what to do." He said sternly.

He wasn't showing me any compassion. I had hurt his girls, and I was keeping the wound open by lingering.

I sucked in a deep breath and moved past him with my head lowered as I met the girls in the lounge. Each stared at me with different emotions.

"Can we take a rain check on the Chinese guys?" I sat beside them on the couch, and they all leaned into me.

"You promise?" Cassie asked.

"I promise! You can call me anytime and we can eat together over Facetime if you want to." I tried to lighten the mood.

"We're gonna miss you." Lilly's face saddened.

"I'm never going to have clean clothes again." Cassie crossed her arms and slumped back.

"HEY! What am I?" Dane laughed.

Cassie smiled at Dane and poked her tongue at him. Tux was resting beside him as Dane brushed through his fur.

"I should go guys, enjoy the day with your dad." I said as I hugged each one and kissed their heads.

I stood up and walked towards the front door and Tux followed me outside.

"WAIT!" Audrey chased me with a jar of dollar bills and fortunes.

Audrey pulled out the fortunes and handed them to me.

"We keep these until the next Chinese meal. It's our tradition. I want you to have them since you won't get your own. Hopefully, they work on you like they did us." She smiled.

I took the fortunes and stuffed them into my pant pocket and hugged her one last time.

"I'll miss you so much." I whispered in her ear and kissed her cheek.

"Thank you for my room." Lilly rushed over and hugged me.

"You are so welcome." I picked her up and squeezed her.

"If you find any weird cereals on your travels, you know where to send them." Cassie winked.

"Come here!" I grabbed her and hugged her.

Cassie was always the one I could count on to lighten the mood and I would miss all her charm and chaos.

She let me go and went to count the dollar bills with Lilly while Audrey hugged Tux.

"I guess this is goodbye." Dane sighed.

"For now…" I nodded.

"You always have a place here, Stella. In any capacity you want." He said as he brushed my hair off my face.

"Thank you for taking a chance on me." I stepped forward and reached my arms around his waist.

"Thank you for helping me find my footing again." He said as he kissed the top of my head.

I stepped back and wiped my eyes and turned to unhook the van. Everything was ready to go, I had a habit of making sure I was ready to move in a minute if I needed to. Tux was inside all ready and sitting on the front seat, he seemed to know what was happening. He perched himself on the window and barked and whined out the window as I drove out of the front yard and down the street. I couldn't look back. If I did, I knew I'd spin around and never leave.

It was me, Tux, and two hours of open road ahead of us as we drove to White Bear Lake.

Dane

The girls raced back inside eager to shut out the past hour and distract themselves with something else. But I stood in the road desperate for her to turn and take one last glimpse. She never did.

I slowly brought myself back inside the house. The girls had already started the movie without me, and I sat down in what was Tux's favorite spot just to get one last whiff of him. When I asked Stella to come and stay with us, I didn't realize the weight of what she would bring into our home. How could someone I didn't know six months ago have me standing in the rain on my street aching for her to see me one last time?

It was clear she didn't feel the same way I did. I knew a part of me was falling in love with her. But not in your typical way. It was for the warmth she brought, the happiness she sprinkled through the little things she did that made life better, the way she could make the girls feel like princesses with a simple coat of paint on their walls or building their bookshelves. She was the main artery of this house.

The weekend seemed to speed past now, we were into another school week and Monday hit harder than normal. I half expected Stella to walk into my classroom but instead, I was assigned an elderly lady who was just as pleasant and sweet, but not someone I could order to take the kids for morning fitness while the moms drank coffee in the carpark that overlooked the oval.

Mark was in his office looking out onto the field as I led the kids out. I could feel his laughter from the window, and I shot him a glare of disappointment.

"Okay guys, two laps around the obstacle course." I blew my whistle.

"Stella only made us do one." Lizzy protested.

"One was the warmup, now it's two." I grumbled.

The kids looked worried as I blew the whistle again and pointed to the starting point.

"I hate this." One kid growled.

"My mom's over there. She'll get me out of this." Another complained.

"It's this or a beep test." I shouted.

"Oh woah!" I heard a mom scowl from a few meters away.

"Okay, let's go." One of the boys nodded at me.

I blew the whistle twice and the kids sprinted off to the obstacle course.

The moms glowered at me with their oversized Stanley mugs of coffee in disgust as I barked orders at their kids as if they were my fellow SEALS.

Mark eventually came out and observed my morning fitness circuit.

"A little harsh?" He asked as he pointed to the kids nursing obvious stitches or panting for water.

"No, they'll have a lot more pain in life than this. Maybe this will teach them to harden up.

"I get that you're hurt, mad even. But you can't come to school and whip the kids for it." Mark said.

"I'm not whipping them." I argued.

"Figure of speech. Take a day off and let it marinate before you come in here and piss off a bunch of parents." He advised.

"I've been *marinating*, I need to be here. I need a distraction." I confessed.

"No, you need to go to take a boxing class and hit something. Your girl left you, your ex-wife's a bitch. You have every reason to be pissed off. I'll come by and watch the kids while you go." Mark offered.

"You serious?" I asked as I ignored the remark about her being 'my girl'.

"I got my baby boy this afternoon, they'll love him." Mark smiled.

"That's awesome, man!" I slapped his back.

"Yeah, Jackson. He's amazing, can't wait for you to meet him. I'll be at your house at five!" he said as he walked off.

He was right, I was being an ass. I was missing Stella and it had barely been two days since she left.

During my lunchbreak, I found myself on YouTube scanning the girl's page for the first video they did with Stella. I just wanted a glimpse of her. Then a notification from Gina lit up my phone and I opened it.

Dane,

I know you don't want to hear from me, but for the girl's sake I'd like to clear the air and hopefully become a part of their lives once more.

I understand I'm not held in anyone's good graces right now, but in time I'd really like to see them for vacations if I can earn their trust back. I commend you for all you've done to breathe life back into our family while I was doing all I could to destroy it. I own that and I'm seeking counselling.

To you, Dane. I'm so sorry, what James and I did is unforgiveable, and we are on uncertain terms of how to move forward.

> Hi Gina,
>
> I appreciate your message and I think this is a positive way of moving forward so you can still have time with the girls. I will have a talk with them on your behalf.
>
> As for your relationship with James I have no ill feelings towards this. You have a baby to consider, and it would be wonderful for him to have both parents around if it's what you both decide, you have my blessing.
>
> For my part in this I deeply apologize.

The message was unexpected but the comfort it brought was welcome. I never wanted a messy divorce from Gina and moving to the most northern state of the country was something I did on a whim not to cause her any distress, which was apparent when she showed up.

The divorce thus far had been pretty simple, we had always agreed to divide everything down the middle and we had stuck to that arrangement.

I'd had the girls almost a year now, this would be our first Thanksgiving and Christmas together without Gina and she hadn't mentioned anything about being a part of it so I trusted that she would take her time with reintroducing herself less aggressively.

Thanksgiving, I didn't have a clue what that entailed. My last five or more had been spent overseas with MREs or on a ship with navy catering.

Mark was across from me hoeing down a chicken and bacon BLT baguette and I kicked him in the leg to grab his attention.

"What do you do for Thanksgiving?" I questioned.

"Eat and then sleep." He laughed.

"Useless." I laughed back.

"Want me to come and cook for you, big guy?" Mark teased.

"Well, actually yes." I chuckled.

"Not a chance." He laughed back.

"I'm going to have to do something seemingly special." I rested my face in my hands.

"You got this, with a name like De La Roche, there's got to be some fancy cooking skills in there." He teased.

"Maybe." I huffed as I stood up when the bell went off for the last class of the day.

Stella

Life was a little colder after I left Duluth and it wasn't because the weather changing, I had lost my will to feel once again. It was the day before Thanksgiving now and I was back to waiting tables at a diner at White Bear for the lunch shift on the weekdays. It was four hours and Tux was back to being miserable with me every time I pulled on that white apron and tied on sneakers not meant for walking him.

"I'm sorry buddy." I hugged his giant face, wiped away his dried tears, and kissed the top of his head.

The sound of kids on vacation was almost like a trigger. Every little girl that squealed I wanted to be Lilly, the tweens with their heads in books reminded me so much of Audrey and I loved interacting with the wild middle children, they were always noticeable, and they weren't ever shy to ask for more breadsticks or extra sprinkles on their ice-cream.

"Stella, can you do the night shift tomorrow?" My boss asked as I walked into the office and put down my bag.

"Yeah, sure." I agreed.

Not like I had any plans or a delicious pecan pie of my own to eat. It had been years since I'd had a slice of my mom's pecan pie. Better yet her derby pie. So gooey and moreish, it was the perfect balance of sweet, nutty, and chocolatey with a perfectly buttery crust.

The pies were all being made today for tomorrow and the smell of pumpkin spice filled the kitchen and every trip I made I stopped a few seconds longer in the kitchen to inhale the smell of freshly cooked food. My kitchen was limited, and I wasn't going to dare create a five-dish meal with one hotplate. The next best option was the Costco premade dinner, the one I'd been eating for years. It was about $40 and meant to serve 8 people. I always made two serves for myself, and Tux got the rest. It was quite possibly his favorite time of year when he would see me coming out of Costco with those heavy trays.

Once my shift ended and Tux had his afternoon walk, I drove to Walmart about ten minutes away and parked under the lights near the surveillance cameras. As long as I had my water filled up and my solar panels fully charged, I was usually good for a few days but made sure to stay on top of these things daily, it always gave me something to do. I started cooking dinner and gave Tux his food and a bowl of kibble along with something chewy to keep him busy.

One more toilet trip and we were looking into the moon and a dark sky, it was time for us to bunker down into bed and watch a movie, but I didn't watch the movie I had put on. I glared at my phone, more specifically Dane's phone number, and hoped he'd call me. Like my gazing would somehow manifest a phone call. I was doing pretty well considering the time that had passed. Three weeks to be accurate and I felt every bit as shitty as I did the day I left.

I still hadn't read the fortunes the girls gave me, so I pulled them out of my drawer of random bits and pieces and sat down ready to read them. The girls had written their names on them, and I unfolded the first one.

The first one was Lilly's, it read '*What good are wings without the courage to fly*'. It was cute considering she had gotten a pair of wings for the Halloween dance, and I knew she'd wear them every chance she got amongst the fairies that were sprayed onto her walls. But in truth Lilly didn't need wings anymore, she had so much courage.

Second was Cassie. '*If you want the rainbow, you gotta put up with the storm*'. Very fitting for Cassie, she had the right attitude to make it through hard times and of all the girls she seemed to have the will to carry on through whatever was thrown at her, she never wavered.

Third was Audrey. '*All the effort you are making will ultimately pay off*'. That felt heavy for a child her age, but maybe it was fitting. She had done a good job at being more of a grown-up at a time when she shouldn't have had to. In turn, it helped Dane and I know she felt peace seeing him at ease.

Last was Dane's. '*Follow what calls you*'. I burst into tears, and I sobbed long and hard. We were so quick to jump each other's bones and lay down rules we never actually gave anything a chance. It was me; I had a damn wall up and now I was numb and the life I was living felt empty and pointless, I had no direction, I had no desire to keep doing this, and yet here I was doing it to prove a point to my dad. Tux hated it too. He missed Dane and the girls; he missed his backyard and the birds he'd made friends with. He probably even missed the random cats that would steal his kibble because he never went outside to eat it. He was what *called* me, and I didn't reciprocate when he had tried more than I deserved.

Fuck, I missed them.

I stared at my phone a dozen more times until the tears blinded me enough to go to sleep.

The next day I woke up as Tux let me know he needed to go to the bathroom. We then walked around and found a spot for a coffee and some breakfast. I didn't normally buy breakfast, but I knew I'd be leaving Tux alone a bit longer today, we deserved to have this time together and he was grateful for the full plate of crispy bacon, sausage, and eggs.

After breakfast, we took a spontaneous swim down the at the Matoska Dog Beach and paddled around with some other dogs enjoying the water on the rare warm day.

Once we were done, I rushed through bathing Tux at the dog wash at a gas station. I towel-dried him enough to bring him into the van where I blow-dried him with the door open so any loose hair would hopefully fly outside and not into the already furry cabin.

Half an hour later and tux was brushed and dry. It was my turn for a shower. I had work in an hour, so I started to hurry. Today was going to be longer and busier, I'd have to try and spread my breaks out so Tux would get enough toilet breaks.

I walked into the already packed diner and my jaw dropped to see the number of turkeys being loaded into the ovens. I had no idea so many turkeys could fit into four giant ovens.

"Stella, I need you stuffing and seasoning those Turkeys, then portion the macaroni into those dishes." The chef ordered.

"Ummm, I'm a server." I gulped. I was overwhelmed by the chaos in the kitchen.

"Not today, I'm two cooks down and I can't trust those teenagers. I need my senior staff in here." He explained.

"Okay, I'll do my best." I nodded. He wouldn't have even seen me he was so busy he was almost hovering off the ground.

I set to work mixing the stuffing and filling the birds with it the way my mom had taught me.

Once they were stuffed, I lathered them in the buttery seasoning already prepared, sprinkled the dry seasonings over them, covered the trays in foil, and placed them in the only free oven.

Next on the list was the macaroni, the trays left out were single serves to be garnished with a fine bacon crumb and placed them in the warmer.

"Stella, can you manage the pies?" Chef asked.

"Sure." I replied as I washed my hands.

I'd never seen so many pies. Pumpkin, Pecan, and Key Lime were the most popular and many were boxed for takeaway orders.

"There's a line out the door for pie pickups. Can you get that under control? They are all pre-ordered." The chef explained.

"No worries." I said as I took the clipboard of orders.

Once I had enough pies boxed it was easier to get the customers out the door and eventually one of the servers was free to help me box them faster.

It was just before the dinner rush, and I took the opportunity to have a quick break and rushed outside to walk Tux a little.

"That's a nice dog." A man smiled.

Tux was unsure of him and kept away even though he normally let strangers pet him.

"He's a bit shy." I brushed it off as him being too cooped up.

The man nodded and walked away from the diner as I gave Tux a plate of food before I put him back into the van. I sat and ate a ham sandwich while I kept my eye on my watch till I had to go back in as people began to scan the area for parking bays and the last of the lunch rush left with their pies after a heavy meal.

My half-hour break passed quickly, and I hugged Tux goodbye as I tucked him back into the van, rolled the lint remover over my clothes several times, and changed my apron.

"See you soon buddy!" I kissed the top of his head and he slumped onto my bed with an irritated exhale.

The kitchen was buzzing once more, and I washed my hands thoroughly before I got started pulling trays of extra stuffing out of the oven.

I was shown how to plate the traditional meals since this was all we were serving tonight alongside a vegetarian version which was simply everything minus the turkey.

The bar was busy and loud as men and women got drunker and drunker, the floors were filthy, and we couldn't clean them fast enough.

The chef finally released me from kitchen duties, and I was able to go out onto the floor to help. Two of the girls were red-faced and close to tears when one man slapped another of the girls on the ass.

"Hey!" I snarled.

"What you gonna do about it?" He stunk of booze, and he appeared disorientated.

"Sir I think it's time we call you a cab." I tried to be assertive, I recognized him as the man who wanted to pat Tux.

"Just one more drink." He slumped into one of the waiting room lounge chairs.

"Of water. Lucy, call a cab please." I whispered to the server behind me.

I handed him a glass of water and he slapped it out of my hand.

"Get out!" One man with a young family stood up and his voice commanded the room with its deep tone. His wife looked worried, and his three kids trembled with fear.

"Damon…" His wife whispered.

"No, this guy needs to learn some manners. Are you okay, love?" He looked at me.

"I'm fine." I nodded.

The drunk guy wobbled as he pulled himself up and tried to land a punch on Damon.

Damon gripped him by the scruff of the neck, he was far taller than the drunk man and hurled him out into the dirt with ease.

"DAMON!" His wife cried. I raced to her side and assured her he would be okay.

Four other men had gone out with them to make sure he left without any further trouble.

Then I heard glass smashing and cars being damaged and the most ear-piercing sound of it all was the howl of an animal in pain, my animal.

I raced outside and the men had the drunk man restrained. He had torn my van open after smashing a window. Tux must have bitten him. Tux was lying on the ground with a puddle of blood around his back hind leg and I fell to his side. He was barely conscious. The knife still sticking out from the top part of his back thigh. There was no telling how long the blade was, Tux was whining in pain.

The man was being held up against my van by all four of the men while others called the police. The drunk man laughed at me as I cried over Tux.

"Someone help him!" I screamed.

Crowds of people rushed out of the restaurant and a handful of them came to my aid with a medical kit and helped compress the wound and keep Tux calm as three people tried to lift him into the back of someone's truck.

"He needs a vet, now!" One yelled.

My eyes were muddy with tears, and I felt like I was floating outside of my body. This can't happen again. Some drunk idiot can't take my best friend…again.

Rage took over me and I smashed my fists into the face of the prick who had hurt Tux, I landed blow after blow, and nobody stopped me. After a while I found myself covered in his blood, his eye so swollen it was likely he couldn't see out of his. I dropped to the ground from exhaustion.

"Come on, let's get you to the vet." A kind woman pulled me up from the ground and handed me a bottle of water.

Lucy raced after me with my bag and hugged me.

"Tell Tux we love him!" She kissed my cheek and gave me a hug I needed.

I climbed into a Silverado I didn't know, and this lady and her husband drove me to the vet where the others had taken Tux. I wept hard for the first few minutes of the drive until she started talking to me and I began to compose myself.

"Sweetheart, is there anyone you need to call?" She asked.

"No…" I sighed.

"Is there anyone who can be with you through this? If not, I can stay with you?" She offered kindly.

"Thank you, there's one person…" I said softly.

For all the Tears we've Shed

Dane

It was Turkey Day. I was somewhat excited I wouldn't be doing this alone. Mark came over with a six-pack of beers and the Costco Thanksgiving kit that was comprised of all the essentials, I remember Stella talking about this and I smiled at the thought of her. The distance between us hadn't gotten easier, but I felt comfort in knowing she was doing something fulfilling with her life.

We put on seasonal movies for the kids while we cooked and chatted about sports throughout the day and played a few board games.

Mark had brought over ingredients to make a Kentucky Derby pie with the girls. They were right into the idea of baking. They began following instructions from an old recipe card that had been photocopied too many times.

Cassie was melting butter. Audrey roughly chopped the pecan nuts and Lilly helped Mark shape the premade pie crust that just needed to be rolled out.

The turkey was finished just in time for the pie to go into the oven and we began serving dinner and did our exchange of things we were thankful for.

I started by saying "I'm grateful for my family, my home, and friends we've made."

Mark reiterated similar notions but reflected warmly on his newborn son and the girls showed enthusiasm to see Jackson again.

Audrey was next. "I'm thankful for my sisters and my dad." She smiled.

"I'm thankful for all of you, my friends, and our new town, it's pretty here!" Cassie said cheerfully.

"I'm thankful Stella washed our clothes; it was good while it lasted." Lilly joked.

"He's getting better." Audrey was quick to protect me.

"Let's dig in!" Mark said hungrily.

We all grabbed slices of turkey and generous servings of everything else. The girls were staying away from the beans, but Cassie took one carrot.

"That pie smells delicious." I complimented them.

"Have you had a derby pie before?" Mark asked.

"I've heard tales that only scratchy recipe cards like yours can hold up to." I laughed.

"Grandma knows best." He laughed. "I had to name my firstborn after her to get that." He added.

" You're joking?" Cassie questioned.

"Nope." He shook his head.

"What was her name?" Lilly asked.

"Jacqueline. My son's name is Jackson." He answered.

"I see what you did there." Cassie winked.

"I did my best.' Mark laughed.

I poured the girl's sparkling apple cider into plastic flute glasses and they cheered as they pretended it was champagne.

"Another?" Mark nodded to the beer.

"I think I'll have one of these." I said as I poured another flute of apple cider.

Mark smiled and grabbed a flute also to try the non-alcoholic option and clinked his glass with the girls.

"That's way better than beer." He laughed.

"I have to agree." I said as my nose inhaled the scent of the derby pie. The oven counted down on the timer and I was eager to try a slice of something sweet and homemade.

Audrey started collecting the empty plates while Cassie and Lilly scrapped theirs off into the bin and rinsed them in the sink before they put them into the dishwasher.

Mark pulled out the pie and left it to cool on the bench while we all rested our stomachs.

It didn't take long until we were all slothing on the couch and falling asleep to Home Alone playing in the background.

I was maybe an hour into my food coma when my phone vibrated loudly on the kitchen counter and the ringtone unsettled Lilly enough for her to throw a cushion at me.

I leaped up and raced to the phone.

'Stella' it said.

I answered the phone and without saying a word she was crying my name in desperation.

"Are you okay?" I rushed to my room, closed the door, and pulled on some boots.

"Tux was stabbed by a drunk patron at the restaurant I work at." She sobbed.

"Fuck." I didn't know what else to say.

"Is he okay?" I pulled myself together and dressed in warm clothes ready to leave instantly.

"I'm at a vet hospital, they are taking him in for surgery." She cried.

"I'm on my way, give me the address." I demanded.

"No, you can't uproot the girls on Thanksgiving." She tried to stop her tears.

"Mark's here, he'll crash the night." By now Mark was in the doorway and we had her on the loudspeaker as he threw jackets at me and signed for me to go and told me it's fine and he'll look after the girls.

"Are you sure?" I asked as I covered the speaker.

"GO! She needs you. Amy is on the way over with Jackson, the girls won't even notice you're gone." He slapped my back. "Go look after the rest of your family." He pulled one side of his lip up into an awkward smile.

"I owe you one." I shook his hand.

"I'm heading out the door now." I said as I grabbed my keys and pecked all of the girls on the head goodbye.

"Thank you." She cried.

"He's going to be okay." I tried to assure her. "Can't say the same for the prick who hurt him." I growled.

"I kind of assaulted him… a lot." She confessed.

"He deserved it." I brushed her off.

"If he presses charges…" She began.

I cut her off at the thought of it. "If he tries, I know a lot of people in high places." I reassured her.

"Thank you." I could hear the tone of her voice relax. "I need to go and check on Tux, I texted the address. See you in a few hours." She hung up the phone.

I sped the whole way there and arrived well under two hours it should have been.

I raced through the front door and the nurse knew immediately who I was there for.

"Dane?" She asked and I nodded. "They are just wrapping up. He did really well. Stella is asleep in that room if you want to go and give her the update." The nurse pointed to a half-closed door.

I pushed the door open, and Stella was asleep on a hospital bed with a thin white sheet covering her legs. Her white apron was splattered with blood. Her hands were swollen, red, and stained with more blood. She had dark circles around her eyes and dirt on her face and in her hair that was crusted with more blood. I brushed her hair off her face, and she shrieked at my touch. Her eyes widened with joy, but she instantly cried knowing it was safe to do with me.

I knelt before the bed with her face in my palms and she climbed down into my lap, and I held her tightly as I explained what the nurse had told me.

"He's almost through it." I wiped her tears away.

"I don't know what I'd do if I lost him. Not like that, not to another drunk idiot." She was angry.

"Stella?" A Dr. knocked on the door and Stella and I stood up abruptly.

"Someone wants to see you." She smiled.

Stella moved quickly behind her as she led us down a corridor full of medical equipment and animal crates.

"He's a bit drowsy from the anesthesia but he should make a full recovery. There was no muscle damage. That bushy coat worked like armor. It was just a big bleeder. Fortunately, the blade was short." She seemed thrilled by the outcome.

"Hey, buddy!" Stella hugged his giant face.

"He still needs to take it easy. He's got twelve stitches, no unnecessary walking and please keep him crated for at least three weeks to make sure that heals properly." The Dr said as she handed Stella a box of painkillers and sheets of paper on aftercare.

"Can we take that crate?" I asked.

"He'll be fine in the van once I get the windows fixed." Stella hesitated.

"No, you guys are coming home." I smiled. " If you'll have me that is?" I questioned.

"I never wanted to leave in the first place." She hugged me.

"We'll take the crate." Stella said as she turned to the Dr.

"It's on the house." The Dr said to the nurse.

We carried Tux out to the truck carefully and placed him in the boot where Stella sat with him the whole way to the restaurant where her van was.

"I'll drive that back. You go with Tux in the truck." I jumped out and snatched the van key from her.

"Do the girls know?" Stella asked.

"Yeah, I got Mark to fill them in.

"He's good peoples." She smiled.

"Amy and Jackson are there too having a little sleepover." I said.

"That's nice, I'm glad they are working it out." She smiled.

"It's trending." I said and sounded immediately cheesy.

She suddenly grabbed my face, pulled me down to her, kissed me, I pulled her up into me and kissed her back gently.

"It's okay if this is temporary, but I hope it's not." I whispered.

"It's not, I'm done. I felt empty the minute I left you all. Everything on all of your fortunes the girls gave me has haunted me. They all felt like they were for me. If you wanna give this another, go. I'd like to date you Mr. De La Roche." She smiled.

" I thought you'd never ask." I laughed.

Stella

Arriving back in Duluth was a comfort in itself. It always felt so homely to me and pulling into the familiar driveway was a breath of fresh air. I hadn't been gone for longer than a month, but it felt like forever. I hadn't lived here any longer than four months, but now that I was back, I never wanted to leave.

As I pulled up, the girls raced outside and tackled me to the ground with hugs.

"We missed you guys, is Tux okay?" Audrey said as hugged me and held on the longest while Cassie and Lilly hurried to the back to see Tux.

"He slept all the way." I yawned.

"Can we help look after him?" Lilly asked.

"Of course, he's, *our* dog." I smiled.

"You're staying?" Audrey screamed.

"If that's okay?" I squinted sarcastically.

The girls huddled into a ball and whispered louder and louder about their achievement and all I heard was *'We did it!'*

Dane pulled in as Mark was walking out with a very tiny baby Jackson.

"Welcome home, Stella." Mark hugged me.

I offered to take the baby and he obliged as I went to check on Tux.

Dane and Mark ordered the girls to open the double doors and Audrey ran inside to layer some towels on the ground where they would place Tux's crate.

They carefully lifted the crate from the car and brought Tux inside and he seemed suddenly at ease to be in the place he knew as home.

I followed my nose inside as I caught whiffs of something sweet. In the kitchen, Amy was serving up slices of a pie.

"Aww, yum! I'm starving." I groaned as I sat on a bar stool across from Amy.

"I heard you've had a bit of a rough night." She handed me a slice and a spoon.

"Do I look that bad?" I laughed. "By the way I'm Stella." I went to shake her hand with the spoon hanging out of my mouth.

"Amy!" She shook my hand and took a bite of the pie also.

I watched over the girls as they fussed quietly and gently over Tux with his door open so they could pat him, he seemed so thrilled to be with them again and nudged his head against their hands softly every chance he got.

"Here buddy, I saved you some Turkey?" Dane leaned down and fed him a big slice of turkey breast.

Mark was putting together a plate of food for me as I yawned over the pie.

"Go shower, you look exhausted." Dane rubbed my back.

"Yeah, I think I might." I said as I quickly ate some turkey and stuffing.

I finished my food, walked down the hallway to the bathroom, and stood in the hot water as I let it wash off the dirt and blood from my wet clothes.

Dane came in soon after and flung the curtain back.

"The idea is to take your clothes off." He sighed as he caught sight of me.

"I missed you so much." I confessed.

"I've missed you too." He nodded.

"I think I might love you, all of you." I cried.

"Just think?" He asked.

"No, I do. I've been so caught up hiding in the past, that I didn't see my future right in front of me." I sighed.

"And you're okay if I have a few strings attached?" He walked closer to me.

"That's what I love most, it's you, it's the girls. You feel like home, nothing has felt like that in a long time." I said.

"Well, I'm glad Estella, because I love you right back." He held his hands at me in a love heart shape, leaned in and kissed my forehead. "I've loved you all along. Since the minute you walked into my classroom covered in Tux's fur." He confessed.

"Why didn't you tell me?" I asked.

"You had to live your life, I had to let you figure it out for yourself." He said.

"Thank you, I've grown a lot because of you." I smiled.

"We'll grow and heal together now." He kissed me beneath the shower.

It wasn't perfect or what I ever imagined love to feel like. It was sudden, fast-paced. It sprung out of nowhere and shook up my life, interfered with all my life choices, and weirdly, I couldn't be happier.

Apparently, I didn't always know what was good for me, somehow my grief over Ana led me to Dane, and Tux's accident was a stroke of fate that made sure we found our way back to him.

The End.

V J Garland